Also by Henry Toledano

The Bitter Seed

The M

NASTY STORIES
AND A FABLE
WITH A HAPPY ENDING

Henry Toledano

IUNIVERSE, INC.
BLOOMINGTON

Nasty Stories and A Fable with a Happy Ending

This is a work of fiction. All of the characters, names, incidents, organizations, and dialogue in this novel are either the products of the author's imagination or are used fictitiously.

iUniverse books may be ordered through booksellers or by contacting:

iUniverse
1663 Liberty Drive
Bloomington, IN 47403
www.iuniverse.com
1-800-Authors (1-800-288-4677)

Because of the dynamic nature of the Internet, any Web addresses or links contained in this book may have changed since publication and may no longer be valid. The views expressed in this work are solely those of the author and do not necessarily reflect the views of the publisher, and the publisher hereby disclaims any responsibility for them.

Any people depicted in stock imagery provided by Thinkstock are models, and such images are being used for illustrative purposes only.

Certain stock imagery © Thinkstock.

ISBN: 978-1-4502-7829-4 (pbk)
ISBN: 978-1-4502-7830-0 (ebk)

Printed in the United States of America

iUniverse rev. date: 12/17/2010

CONTENTS

MADONNA AND CHILD

PRINCESS IS SIXTEEN MONTHS OLD. A sniveling, driveling, whining, little bitch. Tall for her age. Healthy and strong and black. I've never seen a kid with so much energy. She never stops. When she isn't sniveling, driveling and whining she's touching, fiddling, putting her damn little fingers here and there, precisely where they shouldn't be. She wants to play with the paints, brushes, my sketch pad, easel, the pots and jars I have around the place. She drives me nuts the little fart.

"Here's the telephone Princess. You can play with that. Look!" I dial a few numbers, let her listen to the purring and ringing sounds, the weather forecast, the time of day etc. She scowls. She's bored. She prefers pulling the telephone wires. And if not that standing on the table, going into the kitchen, diving into the garbage can, putting everything in her mouth, clanging the saucepans, thumping on the cupboards. As I have just said she never stops. Any normal kid that age sleeps fourteen hours a day. But not this brat. She staggers all over the place. Four eyes are constantly on her. She needs round the clock supervision. Her mother and I are constantly yelling "NO". Our whole conversation is one big "NO". The little beast only screams at us. I would like to clobber her one but I don't dare: she is the apple of her mother's eye. I thank God

I have no children. Her mother is forever shoving things in her mouth (that's the only way you can keep the little wretch quiet) and when she's not doing that she's wiping her tail end. It's a perpetual process. Milk. Honey. Yoghourt, cheese, orange juice. Christ alone knows what goes into that horrid little mouth. Then comes the stench, the shit wiping. Sometimes she stands in the middle of the room and farts, loud and clear, odoriferous. Then she groans, puffs and snorts, contorts her tiny nigger face into grimaces of effort. You know of course she is shitting in her pants. Then comes the ritual of changing her. She is changed around twelve times a day. No peace for the wicked.

Why do I put up with this nonsense?

The short answer is because of her mother. She is just the sort of woman I like. She has long flowing hair, a very slender figure, mercurial bitchy eyes, lips that pout and a stubborn little chin. That's the sort of dish I like. To boot she looks young. I like Lolitas, though she's not exactly a teen-ager. Her age, like mine is indeterminate. I tried to get it out of her, but she wouldn't talk. Top secret. Classified information. I told her I was 31, but I'm actually 44. I don't look it, that's why I can get away with it. All my life I've been chasing pretty young chicks. I sketch and paint them, bed with them. Great. I can't complain. I've never been short of tomato. That is until now. Under doctor's orders I've got to take it easy. I must lose weight, keep more regular hours, drink less, smoke less. He didn't say anything about the other thing, but I suspect he included it. Anyway, I can't gad about as I used to. So I put up with Princess on account of her mother with whom I hope to shack up with for a short time, just until my health is normal again and I can chase around as I used to.

Princess's mother, Joan is white American from somewhere up north, Pittsburgh I believe. She came to The Bahamas five years ago on holiday and has been here ever since. She married a Bahamian, a darkie, but is now separated from him. She says

Bahamians make impossible husbands. She works downtown in Freeport as a shop girl in a photographic art store. That's where I originally met her. She hasn't got much money and I think barely scrapes enough to keep herself and her daughter. (This is where I come in, I hope, for I have a little put aside and as she doesn't appear extravagant could afford to keep her and her brat as well if I must.) On principle she won't take anything from her husband. She hates the bastard she says; calls him a stupid creep, a good for nothing. He used to beat her up and apparently she didn't like being beaten up, that's why she left him. Besides he couldn't hold a job. His only regular income was peddling dope. But he wasn't even a good pusher, he could have earned more, but he was too hooked himself. He'd sampled the lot, from LSD to pot. She didn't know about heroin. The only kicks he hadn't experienced for sure, she claimed, was suicide but soon she suspected he would try that as well. He was it seemed a drag and a dreg, but to me he sounded interesting. What's more it made Joan more intriguing. Lots of white meat drops south for a black bang bang, though at home wouldn't be seen dead with a darkie. This chick however, went one better. She married one of the buggers into the bargain. Metaphorically speaking my hair stood on end. What sort of chick did things like that? She had to be screwy. She simply had to. And you want to know something I get my inspiration from crazy mixed up females. An ordinary girl bores me, anyway after a short while. Joan struck me as being anything but ordinary. Hell I imagined I was in for a ball. I was gleaning all this information the first time she came to my studio — a spacious two roomed affair with patio… We were sitting on the sofa, our four eyes glued to the kid as it staggered, as though drunk, from one prohibited zone to another.

"No Princess… No… NO… NO. NO. NO… Nooooooo."

Oh what the hell. I ignored the little beast. Let her fiddle with the wires. Hope she gets electrocuted. But her mother gathered her up, amid screams and took her on her lap.

"Why did you get married?" I asked.

"I don't know. I had to … I knew it wouldn't work out, but still I had to go through with it… I can't explain."

I shrugged. "And what about her?" I added after a moments reflection nodding in the direction of Princess. "Doesn't he mind not having her? Bahamians are usually very fond of their kids."

She replied cooly: "It's not his. He couldn't have any children."

I was a little taken aback, but nothing really shocks me now. I've been around too long. I pressed on regardless: "And do you know who the father is?" I asked perhaps somewhat tactlessly.

"Of course I do," she snapped. "What do you think I am? I chose him because I wanted him to be the father of my child."

I stared at her incredulously, waiting for her to go on, but she ignored me and turning Princess upside down and pulling her nappy aside examined her backside. "You stink Princess" she said.

I had to wait until the kid was changed. When they came back from the bathroom Joan said that Princess wanted an orange juice, so I had to go to the kitchen to get one.

"Perhaps you had better go and empty the trash can immediately. If you leave her nappy in the house it will begin to smell."

So I went outside and emptied my bin down the main garbage shaft. When I returned Princess was prancing around. Joan was yelling: "Noooo."

"Have you a beer? I'll share one with her and maybe she will go to sleep."

I got a beer out of the fridge.

She drank some beer, but didn't go to sleep. Instead she

stood in the middle of the room and farted. The orange juice was left unfinished.

"And how, as a matter of interest, did you select Princess's father?"

"A bit nosey aren't you?"

"I don't deny it," I smiled."I was just wondering if you wanted another kid and if you needed any assistance…"

She grinned. "You're not married. And you're not black. And you're too fat. And you're not good looking enough. Any child of mine must begin with all the advantages."

"Well thanks for the compliments. I'm sorry I don't fit the specifications. But tell me why must the guy be married and black? I can understand you perhaps being finicky about looks though I do think intelligence is important and you don't even mention it. Perhaps I would pass the IQ test? You said yourself that Bahamians were stupid. Wouldn't you perhaps consider me on other grounds? I do at least qualify in some respects."

I was speaking lightly and in jest, though perhaps not entirely in jest. I dug Joan's slender body and her attitudes were beginning to blow my mind.

But she laughed. She said she liked married men because they caused no trouble. "A married man never wants his child back." She threw Princess a tender look. "She's mine and mine only." She spoke as though she was speaking about her television set. As for the guy being black she was perfectly logical. She dug brown kids! The father she had chosen like a piece of meat at the butcher. He had all the qualities she admired. (See above.) "So you want to screw around?" I told this stud one day. "Okay. Your wife is away. You can screw me. I want a kid by you, But I don't give a damn for you and I don't want you to have anything to do with my child. All I want is your seed.'

"Just like that," I said and I admit I was somewhat stunned.

She nodded. "Just like that."

"No sentiment, affection, love?" I remarked. "I thought women were romantic."

"They may be. But as far as I'm concerned all men are pigs."

I smiled. "That's rather a sweeping statement isn't it?"

"Sweeping but true. All men are pigs." She grinned mischievously. "Present company included."

"You are full of compliments. Are you maybe asking for a little spanking?"

I searched her eyes, but they were cold and betrayed no emotion.

"That's been tried. It does no good. Nothing does any good. I left my husband because he used to beat me up."

"You think then you might have married him in the first place because unconsciously you wanted to be beaten up?"

"Nothing of the kind," she flashed angrily. "Before we were married he was a perfect gentleman."

"Why do you think men are pigs?"

"They just are. They are all the same and only want one thing." … "YOU INCLUDED," she added cattily.

"I don't deny I like you. You wouldn't want to be disliked would you?"

"The matter is indifferent to me."

"I don't believe you. We all want to be liked; perhaps not by everybody but at least some people."

"I like my solitude. There's nothing I'd like more than to live on an island all by myself, with a few kids perhaps, certainly no adults."

"How would you manage for food and the other conveniences of civilization?"

"Everything could be flown into me once a week."

"You are a dreamer,"

"Yes I am. I'm immature… I'm very immature. I can't do anything about it. I am as I am. There's an end to it."

"You're at least honest," I said, "I too am immature. I think all artists are. Unless you look upon the world with the eyes of a child you won't see anything new. That's why I think I paint. It is my way of expressing myself and searching for myself at the same time."

"Bullshit. You paint because you are vain. You want to be exhibited, to have your name on display, because you dislike regular work, regular hours, discipline."

"You certainly dot the 'i's' don't you?"

"I do. I don't believe in lying. I was always telling my husband that! He used to lie so unnecessarily. That's just plain stupid. Of course every body lies, but if you lie you should lie for a purpose, not without reason, though lying in itself might be a good imaginative exercise."

With kind permission from Princess this is what I eked out of Joan in more than ten hours I spent with her that first Sunday she came to my place. For somebody who liked solitude I reckoned I wasn't doing badly. I didn't push my luck however and when I said good night to her at her apartment I didn't even attempt to peck her on the cheek. Play it cool man. The fish always comes to the bait.

"Hallo… Hallo… Peebo.Peebo… Boo…Hee. Hee. Boo. Yes you can ride on my back. Don't pull my hair. Don't scratch my face. Gee-up. Gee-up… Okay. You want me to go faster? Christ Princess you stink. Joan she needs changing. You can punch me in the chest, but not the face. No. No. Ow… I said no. Stop it Princess. Oh, go away you little pest. I'm through with you. All right you can have something to eat. What, you don't like it?… To hell with you kid…"

"I've told you before not to swear in front of her. You're setting her a bad example."

Oh God why am I putting up with this? I'm not a masochist. And yet anybody who puts up with the sort of nonsense I've been stomaching these last three weeks must be. I play with the brat. I suffer its howls, its smells, the systematic destruction of my apartment, not to mention all that's in it… Then I'm black and blue all over. For a toddler she's got the strength of an elephant. And if I don't scream (which she finds funny) she pees on me or worse. All the while Joan encourages her. "Give it to him. Hit him. He's only a man. That's right. That's right. Good. You beautiful baby."

Joan has no use for men. They are an accident of nature, a deliberate mistake. The world would be a better place without them. No, not even their seed is much use. Soon there'll be having artificial insemination with artificial semen.

"Why did you get yourself fucked by a nigger? You could have gone to a semen bank. Plenty around."

She laughed that one off. Not worthy of a reply.

I cook for her. And the kid. I take them to restaurants. Princess in a restaurant is hell. She doesn't only demand our attention but everybody else's — customers, staff, backroom boys, the lot. And what gets me is every body makes such a fuss over the little darling. Why doesn't anybody put a bowl of rice pudding over her head? I at least have the excuse I'm trying to make her mother. Though God knows she doesn't give a thing. She doesn't like being kissed. She doesn't like being touched. She's neither warm nor affectionate. She doesn't stop criticizing me, pulling me to pieces, dissecting my character. I call her the air-conditioner. She says NO, THE DEEP FREEZE. She's got a sense of humor, I'll give her that, even though it is at my expense.

Then I give Joan driving lessons. In my car. Princess sits in the back seat and screams. She pulls her mother's hair and mine. She doesn't keep still for long. She crawls on me, on Joan. I have to pull her away. She grabs a handbrake, the gears the keys. She farts and she pees and she shits. All the while she howls. Like no adult she can concentrate on several things at once. All to perfection. Halleluliah! Then once we went to the movies. For five minutes. Five bucks down the drain. Why can't anybody put her down the drain?

But this is not all. I take them for drives, to the beach, swimming. I do all the carrying and lifting, as well as the thinking. Joan thinks too, but doesn't think it intelligent to think if I'm there to do the thinking for her.

Why do I do it? Why do I do It? I ask myself the question a thousand times. I delve into my subconscious. A waste of time. I like Joan because I like her. She's the apple in the garden of Eden. I want to be the snake, to tempt and lure her, to make her fancy me. I'm trying. I'm trying. Give me my due. I suppose I need a challenge: obstacles and opposition, that sort of thing. Well, I've got them whether I like them or not. And Princess doesn't make things easier. Hell, I'm half inclined to drop the whole business.

I don't however. In fact I'm trying to be extra nice. In my own way I think I'm in love with Joan. I would like to get her out of my system. Or woo her, which would be the same as getting her out of my system. I'm suffering I assure you. On account of her, the kid, my unfulfilled dreams. Particularly my work is suffering. All the chicks I've been trying to sketch and paint recently have been hopeless. I feel I don't even want to do any more work. I am going through one hell of a crisis. I would like to get back to my old self, chasing Lolitas, painting and gadding about. Or better still beat Joan up, tell her to go to hell, boot her out of my life. My mental health is deteriorating. Ditto my physical health. The doctor has told me to lead a quiet life. Don't get excited, he says. He's given me vitamins, tranquillizers, pills of various shapes and sizes. I don't know what is wrong with you, he says: take it easy.

I KNOW WHAT IS WRONG WITH ME.

"Good night Joan. Let me give you a kiss, just this once. It's the last time I'll be going out with you. I'm fond of you but you're just too much for me."

"If that's a trick to get a kiss out of me, it won't work." And she pulled away.

"You're a real bitch," I said staring at her yearningly.

"You like bitches," she replied teasingly.

"There are limits."

Princess sprayed my trouser bottoms with hair spray. I kicked her.

"Don't be rough with her," protested Joan.

"I'm sorry."

"You'd better go."

"I'm going. Good night." At the door I stopped. "Not even one kiss?" I enquired and I think it might have been beseechingly.

"GO MAN. GO."

"Bitch."

A few days later I dropped round at the shop where she worked. She was dressed in red, trousers and all. Trousers made her look very elegant, sexy. She had that sort of figure. When she saw me she beamed. I actually felt she was pleased to see me.

"Are you hungry?" I asked.

"Starving."

"How about lunch?"

"Fine."

She stopped what she was doing immediately and, gathering up a parcel from under the counter, led the way out. As soon as we were away from the shop she handed me the package. "A present for you," she said.

"What is it?" I took the paper bag and peeped inside. There were rolls of film, tubes of paint, one or two brushes and other photographic and art knickknacks.

"Compliments of the management," she smiled.

"Did you pinch them?" I asked.

"Of course I did, You don't think I'd pay for them do you?"

"Won't they get mad?"

She snorted. "The boss is an idiot. He hasn't a clue what

he's got. All the girls steal. We'd be foolish not to with the salary he pays us. He's a horrible little man. He deserves what he gets. I've never seen such an inefficient organization in all my life."

I thanked her. For lunch I took her to the pub on The Mall. During the meal she complained about the job, how she hated it — the other girls, the boss, the customers, everything connected with it. She wasn't built for that kind of work. The clientele was stupid, coarse and rude. She felt like telling it to get stuffed. She didn't because of Princess, though if she got fired she didn't really care, for she could get a job anywhere.

"Though I've got no special qualifications I can do more than these stupid Bahamians. My boss knows that. That's why he'll think twice before getting rid of me. He hates me taking my lunch break when I please. And returning when I please. He doesn't like that at all."

"Still, I'd watch your step if I were you. You never know what he'll do."

"Oh, I don't suppose I'll stick the job much longer. I hate nine to five anyway. I'll probably go back north soon. I'm sick of The Bahamas. Though God alone knows what I'll do. You don't know how lucky you are to be independent."

"Perhaps you'll get married," I said encouragingly. I felt sorry for her.

"I'm married now."

I laughed. "So you are, I was forgetting... Maybe you'll find a man to provide for you?"

She grinned. "I'm looking. Preferably he should be over ninety and leave all his money to me when he dies."

Then I don't know what came over me. All my resolutions down the drain. It just came out: "How about shacking up with me Joan?" There's a spare room. It wouldn't cost you anything... I'm not rich, but I could keep you... and Princess in modest comfort. You wouldn't have to do any work. You could look after Princess, me... putter around, do what you please. Your time would be your own, subject of course to the dictates of that little pest of yours… What do you say?"

She didn't answer at once, but looked straight at me, as though through me.

"Come on, say YES."

"Yes."

I beamed. "Fine. When do you move in?"

"Tomorrow first thing. I'll quit the job this evening."

When I left her I felt great. I knew I had won.

Christ Almighty. I'm going mad. Joan and her little black bastard have been with me a month. I don't get a moments peace. Princes goes to sleep at 10.00 and wakes (including neighbors) at 6.00… I have to get her milk, warm it, bathe her, see that she doesn't make any noise, for Joan likes sleeping late… What I do to keep the little brat quiet. She's got 'carte blanche' with my paints. She can scribble and color to her black heart's content, whenever and wherever she wants. Then I make faces at her, give her piggy-back rides, let her beat me up. God knows what I have to stomach from the monster. And naturally I am constantly stuffing goodies in her mouth.

That's not all. The driving lessons are continuing. I'm teaching Princess to swim, talk — say "MAMA". That drives Joan round the bend. (I do it deliberately.) She hates being reminded she's a mother, though she loves being one. Screwy, but that's how she is. And I take them for drives, to the beaches, restaurants, shops and all the while I am footing the bill. Money straight down the drain. Dwindling all the time. I'm worried, very worried. Joan doesn't give a damn. I suppose when I can't afford her any more she'll just pick up her bags and go; without so much as a thank-you. She's a first rate scrounger. I have no illusions about that. Bloody bitch.

I'm not sleeping properly. I'm not eating properly. I've got nervous headaches. I'm irritable, moody, very frustrated. My stomach is giving me hell. My digestion is all up the creek.

I'm a storehouse of aches and pains. And complaints. I get no sympathy from Joan. Nothing. Not even one lousy peck on the cheek. Nurse-maid, porter, bank, garbage can—that's me. In her eyes only a man. She's got me where she wants. In her presence I'm like a lump of putty. I've got no personality at all. Once I did grab hold of her. All I wanted was a little hug (nothing wrong with that), just a whiff of affection. She stood perfectly still. She showed no reaction at all. I got the impression I was holding an iceberg and one which was so cold that it wasn't even melting.

Then I got mad. I pushed her away and began yelling: "You bloody bitch. You don't deserve me. I'm too good for you. What you need is somebody to beat you up. And… and I'm going to get myself stoned, stinking drunk and when I'm stinking drunk I'm going to beat the living daylights out of you."

She laughed. I slammed the door behind me.

I went and got myself drunk that night but it was the most peaceful night I'd had in ages, for I slept late and when I awoke Joan had already attended to Princess. I got merry hell I can tell you that. It was as though we were married. But I was still high and laughed.

"Why don't you go to the toilet Joan. Jump down the hole. Pull the chain. And whatever you do don't forget to take Princess with you."

I roared my head off. She ignored me.

A few nights later, however, things came to a head. I stormed out of the house and went to the movies. We'd had a minor row, but I was all on edge and couldn't take any more. The pictures, I hoped would change my ideas. But they didn't and I walked out after half an hour. I dropped in at the pub and had a drink, then returned to the apartment. I let myself in and went to my room. Princess was asleep on the bed.

Without knocking I bounced in the adjoining room. "What the hell is Princess doing in my room on my..."

The sentence was left unfinished. Joan was on the bed naked and next to her some black, also without a stitch — a guy I'd never seen in my life.

"Get out," she hissed.

"You fucking little bitch," I cried and flung a fist at her.

The darkie blocked the blow: "Hold it man," he protested.

"You mind your own bloody business," I yelled. "And get out." And I grabbed his clothes which were on the chair and hurled them into the corridor.

He seized me in some Judo grip. All these black Bahamian bastards seem to know Judo. He instructed me to pick his things up and put them back on the chair. When I refused he twisted my arm until I squealed... and agreed. He let me go.

Joan beamed. "Why don't you beat him up Ding. Bash him."

"He ain't done nothing man."

"He doesn't like niggers."

He grabbed my neck this time. He shook me. "Get out. We ain't done yet."

"You get out," I screamed, shaking myself free and withdrawing a pace. "This is my house and I have in it who I please."

"Hit him," said Joan.

"Don't you dare," I threatened. "If you so much as touch me you'll regret it. Both of you will."

He laughed. They both did, He took a step forward and I took a step back.

"I've warned you," I cried. "Don't try anything."

This time his laughter was forced. Somehow my tone was getting through. He was bigger than me and stronger, but I was mad — my adrenaline was flowing and he knew it.

"Go on Ding give it to him."

Before he had time to take another step forward I dashed into my room and snatched Princess off the bed, who promptly began screaming and kicking. "GET OUT OF HERE WHEN I TELL YOU," I thundered.

He paused and looked awkwardly from child to Joan. She had gone white.

"You'd better go Ding," she said softly.

Sulkily he gathered up his clothes. He mumbled a few threats and curses as he went out, but I didn't pay attention. I told him to bang the front door when he left. The brat was still howling and wriggling in my arms.

""Now you bitch," I turned to Joan. "I'm going to deal with you. I've just about had all I can take from you, you filthy slut, You make me sick. I don't know what I saw in you."

"PUT HER DOWN."

"This… This bit of dung," I said holding Princess high above my head. I dropped her. Then tried to catch her in mid air, but missed and she fell on the bed screaming louder than ever.

"YOU BASTARD, YOU BASTARD," hollered Joan trying to tug my hair. I threw her down on the bed, but she fell on the floor. I grabbed up Princess again. Ding bounced into the room, half dressed (obviously aware of the commotion), but when he saw I still held the baby he hesitated. "Ah… ah… Don't you dare," I warned. "I told you to get out. I don't want to see you again."

This time I followed him into the lounge where he had been dressing. I watched him put the remainder of his things on in silence. Joan joined us a few seconds later staggering into some trousers.

"PUT MY BABY DOWN," she yelled.

I laughed. "What did you want this time? Another fuzzy-wuzzy?"

Ding hurled himself at me and would have sent both me and the infant flying if Joan hadn't had the presence of mind to jump between us. "No, no Ding," he's mad. He's capable of anything. He might kill her."

"Damn right I might. Listen to the little lady. For once she's talking sense."

Ding left us slamming the front door behind him. Joan looked petrified. I stared at her. Princess screamed and kicked. I held tight.

"Now my dear girl I'm going to have my fill. Go back into the bedroom. Take those things off and lie on the bed."

She didn't move.

"Do what I say."

When I went into her bedroom a few seconds later, still holding Princess, she was waiting for me as instructed.

"I'm going to rape you," I said cooly.

"You're mad."

"Yes, mad to have put up with you for so long. Now you're going to get what you deserve. What you've been asking for all the time."

"If you touch me you'll go to prison."

"What for?" I laughed,

"You said you were going to rape me," she stammered.

"And so I am. But what Jury would convict a man for raping the girl he is living with? You'd better think of something better than that."

"I didn't make any promises when I came here." Really I thought she was being a remarkably brave girl. She was certainly putting on a bold front.

"Yes, that's true," I conceded. "But when you agreed to move in I took your silence for acquiescence. But enough talking. You've never appreciated my talk."

"What are you going to do with her?" She nodded towards Princess, fear in her voice.

"Nothing at all. She can watch if she likes."

"You... you... you bastard. Listen. I beg you. I'll do

whatever you say, but put her down. Leave her in the other room. I'm begging you. Please."

She actually got down on her knees in front of me.

There was an evil smirk on my face. I grinned: "I don't trust you." I said cooly staring down at the prostrate figure.

"I beg of you, please. I'll do whatever you want."

"You should have thought of that earlier."

She started fiddling with my fly,

"Really I don't see what you're worrying about. She might enjoy watching. Besides, what difference does it make? I doubt if the experience would be traumatic. After all with such healthy parents as you and that black you carefully vetted for the job I shouldn't think anything would disturb her."

"You're evil."

I don't think I am however, for I did what she asked and took Princess into the next room. When I returned Joan was on the bed as before. I started undressing,

For a long time he just stared at the canvas. Instinctively I felt it was the best thing I had ever done. After Joan and Princess had left the next day a daemon possessed me and I set to work with fury, letting the mood guide me along, as though I was the instrument and not the brush. Pots and pans, milk, cheese, yoghourt, wrapped in Kleenex, or toilet paper, messy, bound with telephone wire— one end to the receiver, the other around a baby's neck, mouth open dripping chocolate mousse, bloody hamburger. Nude woman part black, holding baby's body (head decapitated) throwing it into trash can. Steering wheel in her other hand. An apple tree, snake coiled asleep. The colors are vivid and startling: bright yellow, orange, deep brown. The picture is really impossible to describe. It's too symbolic, impressionistic. It has to be seen. It is now being exhibited at _____.

"I like it. I like it" said the expert judiciously. "Morbid, morbid. Pathological. It reeks of aggression. I get a restless feelings, a sense of utter frustration. But good, good. I like it though I don't know if I like the name. A bit of irony on your part eh? Well, we can always call it some thing else."

"I don't think I want to," I replied. "I like MADONNA AND CHILD."

He looked at me oddly, his eyes softened a little: "You suffered a lot, yes?"

I nodded.

"Ah… such humiliation, despair." He shook his head. "I see a very tormented soul… Anger. Much anger." He mumbled some more but was inaudible.

What he would never know, nor would anybody except Joan, was the crowning humiliation, that — that, at the crucial moment there had been no desire.

BERT

I met him at college my second term. He was sitting opposite me in the cafeteria chewing apple pie and custard. It was late and nobody else was around. We started talking. I don't remember what about. I was too busy summing him up. He sort of spoke like a computer, unemotionally, softly, Conscientiously: The tone was one of infallibility. But he didn't only speak like an oracle he looked like one. He had a long pale face, fair hair, powerful spectacles, so that when you looked through them the eyes, which were cold and piercing, appeared small. His cheeks were baggy, the forehead high, lips thin, chin receding. Bert looked a bit like a fish with a big head and no tail. "I'm all brain," he described himself as though nothing else mattered. He wore shabby grey flannels and his sport jacket had patches at the elbows.

Bert was a student, a student of human nature. Everywhere he went he studied. He studied people by looking at them. He spent hours in cafes, refectories, snack bars — eating places of one description or another. When it was fine he walked about the streets, sat in the park, had a ride on top of a bus. To be sure he always lugged some books around with him. Whether he ever opened them I don't know, but they were always changing. Bert flitted from topic to topic much in the same way as a fly never settles for long. "My trouble," he used to explain to me "is I haven't yet found my subject." When he did, he went on, there was no knowing what he might do. I got the impression he was another Leonardo. Coolly he informed me he had the IQ of a genius. But being a genius wasn't an easy job. Nobody understood genii, except when they were dead. He bore his cross as bravely as possible. He couldn't concentrate very well due to certain emotional blockages which he was trying to work his way through. His parents were ordinary middle class, rather silly people, conventional, staid, humdrum. "All they think of is keeping up with the Jones. They're disappointed I'm a genius. They think I should be respectable, earning a living, married with kids." What Bert was trying to say, I think, was that he had been mishandled, misunderstood, mis-everything else. At the time I was 20; he was 29. He had passed no exams, was rejected by the army, had never done a day's remunerative work in his life. He lived with his parents (board and lodge provided) and was given 5/- pocket money a day. I extracted all this information from him in less than a week of knowing him.

Bert I thought was a freak, but because I was a little unsure of my opinion I took him along to meet Cyril and Rita, a middle-aged couple I'd known since first coming to London. We sat around the room staring at each other like debutantes at their first dance. Now and again there was an attempt at polite conversation. "What do you do Bertrand?" "I'm a student." "What do you study?" "Knowledge." "'What is your particular field?" "I don't draw a distinction between one field and another. All knowledge overlaps." "What exams are you going to take?" "Those I put my name down for." Cyril laughed a little. "What plans have you for the future?" "To carry on working." "But how do you propose to earn your living?" "Through my work." "But you haven't told us what it is." Here I broke in: "Bertrand is a student of human nature." Cyril grunted noncommitally, then pointing to the books on Bert's knees asked what he was reading. "Compulsion and Doubt by Stekel." "What's the other book?" "Waite's Compendium of Natal Astrology". "You're not interested in astrology are you?" said Cyril in a tone of voice implying only lunatics were interested in it. "I'm very interested in astrology," replied Bert. "Who knows one day I may be an astrologer." "Cyril threw me and his wife an odd look. He switched the talk to other things — current affairs, personalities, sport, this and that. Not a word from Bert. "Aren't you interested in these things?"asked Cyril. "There's no point," replied Bert. "What do you mean?" "They're all transient. I'm only interested in the eternal. What's the use of learning something if it's not going to last?" Again Cyril threw me and his wife an odd look. There was a pause and Rita served us tea. Bert sipped obstreperously and when he munched the toast he made a loud pumping sound.

When we left the Nessims Bert gave me his opinion. Cyril, he thought, was intelligent. "You can see he's an able man." Over Rita he went into ecstasies: "She's delightful, charming, intelligent too. She must have been very pretty. She's not bad now." I said nothing, but I was shaken, for I found Rita a bore, stupid, ugly; though at the time I didn't know her too well. "Tell me Bertrand," I pursued. "Don't you feel a bit bad being 29 and not being able to pass any exams or earn your own living?" He looked at me with a little air of surprise. "No; why should I?" "Well, I mean, damn it all, at your age most people are settled, in a job with a wife and kids. Don't you feel out of it somehow?" "I'm not in the rat race," he answered. "I'm studying in my own way and in due course I'll make my contribution to human knowledge." "How can you be so certain?" "I'm not. Nothing is certain. But it is written in the stars," and he tapped the book he was holding: "One day I shall be famous and great." "You don't believe that rubbish do you?" He gave me an angry look. "It's not rubbish. Just because astrology isn't an exact science now doesn't mean it never will be. In the time of Heraclitus physics and chemistry weren't exact sciences." I changed the subject: "Don't you think Bertrand?" (At this stage of our acquaintance I always called him Bertrand. He liked it that way because he could identify himself with Bertrand Russell.) "Don't you think Bertrand," I repeated, "that if you put more effort into your work you'd do much better?" He replied: "Academic work should be spontaneous. If I made any effort all my energy would go in effort instead of thought." This was the sort of talk I had with Bert when I first met him. At the time (as I've already said) I was unsure of myself, what I was going to do, my future — that sort of thing. Bert intrigued me because he appeared to have no prospects, no means of livelihood, nothing to look forward to and yet, for all that, he didn't seem to worry or care a damn. His indifference was something I would have gladly emulated.

That same evening I rang the Nessims. Rita answered. Before I had time to even ask she blurted it out: "Where did you fish such a character?" She had no need to say more. Her opinion and Cyril's was no different from anybody else. And, as though that wasn't enough, Bert knew precisely what people thought and said of him. But somehow he didn't mind, or that was the impression he gave, the burden he had to bear. He was a little sorry for his contemporaries. "They know no better," he quoted Christ. Don't get me wrong, Bert wasn't a Christian. On the contrary he had a profound contempt for all religions, especially organized ones, which he claimed were political parties with different names.

I must confess (though I never had the courage then) that Bert became my friend. When I got to know what people thought of him I kept him to myself. If we happened to crash into anybody I pretended I'd just met him. If any of my more respectable friends asked whether I was still seeing that nut Bert, I laughed disparagingly and said: "I avoid him like the plague, but he insists on following me around everywhere".

The truth is we saw quite a lot of each other. We went for walks in the park, had rides on buses together, roamed the streets, saw pictures, frequented dives and much else. Sometimes he came to my place. Once and once only he took me to meet his parents. We had crumpets, tea, cake. His parents were Victorian, old, genteel, respectable. You got the impression Bert was an accident, the only accident, for they had no other children. I mention all this because I got involved with Bert emotionally speaking. Without doubt I was his nearest approximation to a friend. His role in my life was a different one. He fulfilled a need which I can only describe as a desire to feel superior. I felt a worthless worm. I was constantly berating myself. I was loaded with sin. Sometimes I contemplated suicide. Bert being around somehow reassured me that I couldn't quite be rock bottom. If I was a worm he was the slime on which I crawled.

Our relationship developed gradually in, I think, a little over a year. At first my demands were tentative and merely in jest. I never paid Bert anything. In return for his services — cleaning my shoes, tidying my room, arranging my papers, etc, (none of which, incidentally, he did properly). I took him to the pictures, gave him a meal, bought him a book or two. To be sure the little favors I did for him included permission to be exacting, insulting, unreasonable in one way or another. Now and again I would kick or punch him, but never very hard as I was frightened he would leave me altogether, something I couldn't face at the time. When payment in kind became payment in cash I don't exactly know; all I know is it did. And from then on I saw more of him. I think at one time I was seeing him almost daily; I had to beg to see him. He got up around mid-day, had a snack lunch at home prepared by his mother and then took the tube to town. (He lived in Tottenham.) He came to town ostensibly to work. I got the impression he never did any. No matter. The fact is that whenever I suggested anything—a walk, pictures, museum, what have you — he was busy, masses of work to do. What used to get me is the one-sidedness of our relationship. He didn't seem to care a damn for me. He practically never phoned me and when he did it was either to ask me a favor or borrow money. His indifference infuriated me. Nor did he appear to be humiliated by some of the tasks I gave him. He did them, then asked for the cash. "Don't you think that cleaning my shoes is beneath you?" I used to ask him. "No, why should I? I'd only feel it beneath me if I was inferior, but as I'm superior it doesn't worry me in the least." The extraordinary thing about Bert was he was just as contemptuous of everybody as everybody was of him. On one occasion I questioned him about this: "You look upon people as though they were dirt. Do you realize that most people think you're somewhat less than dirt?" "They may do." he replied; "but whereas one day I shall be an important man, they will merely be bankers, clerks, teachers, something quite lowly anyway." At this I laughed. How deluded can you get, I wondered.

To be sure I imagined Bert was a man without a future. When we went away for our summer holiday (it was 1954) I became convinced of the fact. For three and a half weeks I saw nothing but Bert. I got to know him through and through. (This was the first time I'd lived with him.) We drove down to Portugal and I did the driving as he couldn't drive.

The fun started as soon as we stopped that first night at a hotel. Bert didn't want to share a room with me. The only explanation he gave was he'd never done it before. (Of course he didn't have much say in the matter as I was footing the bill.) Actually I soon discovered the real reason why he didn't want to share a room with me. It was on account of his ritual. For three and a half weeks, morning and night, I had to witness exactly the same ceremony. After the first day he didn't exhibit the slightest embarrassment and I came to view his ablutions as no more peculiar than the occasional visit to the barber.

As soon as he woke up, which was usually late, he jumped out of bed, stripped and placed himself in front of the largest available mirror. Imagine the scene then! There he is starkers in front of the looking glass. The sight isn't very gratifying. Bert, though only 31, has quite a paunch and his chest is flabby like a woman's breasts. His behind is long and fat. Nor has he much hair on his body, except between his legs. He looks like one of those Sumo wrestlers — tall, slimy, bloated. He begins his ceremony immediately, as soon as he has positioned himself in front of the mirror. Carefully, with the utmost delicacy, he examines his private parts and makes quite sure they are spotless. He has some lotion or other which he uses to spray himself. (I never discovered what it was.) When he was done he powders himself. Meticulously he caresses talcum over his balls and pats some onto his behind. Covered in white his bottom looks like an alabaster sculpture. But this is only the beginning. Next he sprays deodorant under his armpits. (The deodorant has a little smell, not unpleasant and I suspect it was this that Rita referred to when she said he smelt). Then comes the longest part of the ritual. This consists in scrupulously examining his face, as tenderly as he had previously inspected his balls, and squeezing whatever pimples he can find. He's still nude in front of the looking glass, but now he has affixed his personal mirror, one that magnifies, to the larger glass. Everything is thought out beforehand. The personal mirror is the sort that sticks to any smooth surface as it has one of those rubber suction devices. I forgot to mention he shaved (a wet shave) before going to bed at night. He seemed to think this gave him a hairy look by morning and made him appear more virile during the day. That's what he told me anyway. When he's satisfied his face is clear of pimples (sometimes this takes the whole morning) he massages it with eau de cologne and then gently smears it with face powder. All this was in the morning. At night he puts cream on his face; the idea being it soaks in while he is asleep. The ritual in front of the mirror completed

a few other things too if only I could remember them. I really had an excuse when I didn't take his latest aspirations seriously. "That's a nice useless subject," I commented, "you should be admirably suited to it".

Bert was an enthusiast, anyway, for a day or two. The first thing he did was to cast his own horoscope. As might have been expected he prophesied a brilliant future for himself. He told me he was a genius because his Mercury, Uranus, Neptune were in favorable aspect, whatever that might mean. The only bad aspect in his chart was Saturn, which tended to produce delay. "But there are so many good factors that in the long run that won't matter," he said. "What about your love life?" I asked bitchily. Fuck me, he's even optimistic about that: He prophesied a brilliant marriage for himself — youth, beauty, wealth, the lot. "Do you believe all that stuff?" I retorted. "Sure I do," he replied with conviction. "If it's written in the stars what will be will be." I laughed, then did him the honor of letting him cast my horoscope. You know what he said, the bastard. As a special favor, because I was his friend he'd do it, free this time, but only the once; in future I'd have to pay. About my prospects he was far from optimistic. He told me I was about to fail an exam. I wasn't as bright as I thought I was. An old woman would come into my life. In time I would get married. My job would never be exciting. I'd never be as great or famous as him. I found his predictions so funny and so out of tune with reality that I split my sides laughing.

The way I gained a further insight into Bert's character is I fear equally well a reflection of my own impropriety. The only excuse I have is at the time I was just 22. I refer to how I discovered about his sex life. Before going to Portugal, outside masturbation, I assumed he didn't have one. Bert, I suspected, was a virgin, for the very good reason I couldn't imagine any woman sleeping with him. I knew what some of the girls at college thought of him. He knew too. It wasn't flattering. The kindest remark I heard a girl make was he had no sex appeal.

One or two of the boys suggested he wasn't interested in sex; possibly he was impotent. We speculated a good deal on Bert's sex life. (This was before I got really involved with him.) At the time most of us were interested in psychology and we genuinely believed you couldn't really know a person until you knew something about his sex life. My first few days living with Bert I became convinced he was just as attracted to girls as the rest of us. He liked commenting on them as they passed in the street. Sometimes he would ogle at them, so much so that I felt embarrassed. "Is this what being on holiday does to you?" I asked him. "The girls in England are dreadful." he replied. "I like women to be feminine. Those in England are like Amazons." Once or twice back in London I had taken Bert to a dive. It was always a job to get him to go (he said they were a bore) and in the end he only came because I paid him. Why I took him was a different matter. I think there were several reasons: I wanted company; I felt secure if there were two of us; I liked to boast a little, show Bert what a hit I was with the women, but the real reason I wanted him was out of perversity: I wanted to see how he reacted in such an environment, would it sex him up? As things turned out I was always disappointed, nothing ever happened, Bert couldn't dance and he just sat, quite unemotional, sipping some sort of fizzy drink. He was no different from sitting in the park; he could have been observing butterflies. I mention this as it was the prelude to getting to know about his sex life.

I think it was the third or fourth day I got the idea. "I'm feeling a bit randy, Bert; how about going to a brothel?" "I don't like paying for that sort of thing." "I'm not suggesting you do. I'll do the paying." "Oh." He paused to consider the proposition. "Why don't we pick up a couple of girls in a café?" he eventually suggested. "No point, they're Catholic; you won't get anywhere with them." Again he pondered my argument. To cut a long story short he agreed to come to a brothel. I hailed a cab and though I couldn't speak Portuguese the driver quickly understood what we wanted. It was a posh house he took us to. "Viente chicas," he grinned. And soon they were parading in front of us, most of them beautiful to look at. Bert and I were comfortably ensconced in arm chairs. Out of the corner of an eye I watched him closely. He seemed in no hurry to make a choice. "Well,'"I said. No reaction. I pressed him further. He sighed as though I was boring him. Pause. "Choose one for me," he eventually whispered. I pointed to the ugliest girl in the room, fat, greasy. "What do you think of her?" His eyes lit up. "Smashing," he replied. I nodded to the girl and quickly picked one for myself. The Madame understood a little English and I hurriedly told her what I really wanted. She didn't seem surprised. She smiled comprehendingly and nodded; presumably such requests were all in a day's work. What I had told her was I didn't want a girl for myself, but wanted to see Bert perform.

He was shown into the special room. I took up my position at the spyhole. I see the whole thing very clearly: It is as though it is happening now. Bert is sitting on the bed, The girl has introduced herself as Lolita and is snuggling close to him. He is looking dumb like a tortoise. Unmoved. A few moments go by, then she suggests they get undressed. No sooner said than done. She isn't wearing much and in a trice she is naked. Bert has had time to remove one shoe. The girl is not only fat, greasy; her breasts sag; she has had a Cesarian. Certainly the ugliest of the bunch I conclude. There she is them standing nude in front of him. Her very hideousness seems to excite him. He grabs her buttocks and breasts, but she gives a tiny squeal and he relapses into his shell again. Slowly he strips, neatly arranging his clothes on the chair as he does so. Lolita, in broken English is offering her menu, how does he like it? Front-ways, sideways, ass-ways? No response. Bert is now in his underclothes. He's removing his vest. Lolita continues: In her mouth, between her titties, up her behind? Bert is a bit shy about removing his underpants. Lolita is staring at him a little perplexed. An odd fish, she seems to be thinking. "Photographs; vibrator, spanking, whipping, *soixante-neuf*... mama mia, what do you want?" Bert's reply almost makes me piss in my pants. "I just want to look at you." he says. "No fuckes?" asks the flabbergasted Lolita. He shakes his head. "Show?" she suggests. He smiles guiltily. He's still in his underpants. No attempt to remove them. His erection is small. "Blaspheme," he says. Of course it's quite useless, she doesn't know what the word means; and even if she did her English isn't good enough. Bert starts talking to himself. He's using vile language. Among other things he wants a bottom and titties competition, the girls lined up, parading like when we first came in. The winner to get a slap and kiss on the behind. He got his biggest kick from the parade, he says. The girls should have been nude. (I suspect he came during the line-up. Why else wouldn't he take off his underpants?) Meanwhile Lolita, quite oblivious of what he is blabbering about, walks up and down in front of him. This goes on until there is a wrap on the door. Time is up!

Poor old Bert, I thought, doomed to frustration. Where would he find money for parades of girls who blasphemed beautifully? Foreign girls to boot, as he didn't like English ones. No doubt to really satisfy him he needed to be a millionaire, sultan of a harem, a very special kind of harem — overseas graduates, Oxford naturally, with Firsts in English! All this I felt was asking too much. No matter. As far as I was concerned my knowledge would give me a trump card.

Shortly after coming back to London Bert began to have trouble at home. His allowance was cut to zero. His parents seemed to think if they gave him nothing he would be forced to find work. Certainly they didn't know him very well, for that was the last thing he intended to do. The effect of having his allowance eliminated was he scrounged more off his friends. And as yours truly was his closest approximation to a friend I was the only person to give him anything regularly. The rest of his acquaintances soon got sick of him and after a while wouldn't even speak to him. Rita and Cyril were kind to him because they felt sorry for him. They didn't give him money, but he had a knack of turning up just as they were about to start a meal. Being generous people they always invited him to join them. And the kinder they were the more Bert granted them the privilege of his company. (He was under the impression they liked him.) Often when I used to go round to see them he was already there. Now and again (of course when Bert wasn't around) they'd lecture me: "You oughtn't to see him. He's a bad influence. He keeps you away from your work. And we suspect you give or lend him money. If you do, that's wrong. When you're earning your own living that'll be a different matter. You'll be able to do what you like then. But at your age one doesn't know the value of money. Your father didn't leave you his wealth to waste on a man like Bert." This kind of talk kept me mute. I liked Rita and Cyril, but couldn't explain to them my emotional hang-up, my attachment to Bert. (They wouldn't have understood anyway). Besides, I didn't think they were being that consistent in their own behavior. Why were they putting up with him? But I knew they were right — Bert was costing me too much. And to make matters worse as the pressure increased at home (the family was driving him mad, he said) he began to step up the financial pinch on me. He wanted to come and live in town. On several occasions he told me outright I should give up my room and share a flat with him. "You haven't the dough," I would answer bluntly. "I will have when I get a job." "When that happens ask me again." "You could lend me some in the mean time. You've got plenty. I don't know why you're so mean. You can't take it to the grave." I would protest and tell him I wasn't a blinking millionaire. But he never took my explanations seriously. The status quo continued.

A little before Christmas he adopted a different approach. He suggested if I wouldn't move he'd share my room with me. Naturally only until he found a job. Hesitantly I agreed he could stay with me until the end of the Christmas holidays. "Then out you go, job or no job." A day or two later I went to Tottenham to collect him. He took it for granted I should be his porter and driver. (He claimed he couldn't manage his baggage on his own.) He moved into my place as though it was a hotel. No sooner had I recovered from helping him haul his trunk than his demands began. Would I clear a cupboard so he could put his things away. Then he wanted towels, sheets, a space in the bathroom. And I must remember to be quiet in the mornings, not to draw the curtains because he slept late. Then blow me he wanted to know the set up when he found a girl, for fucking. I snorted and told him the question was academic. As for linen I said he should have brought his own. But when I realized he might use mine anyway I gave him what he wanted.

Of course the obvious happened. The end of the holidays came and Bert hadn't even started looking for work. Blandly he assured me he wasn't disturbing me. My trouble was I was lazy. What was to stop me studying in the library, he wanted to know? It was no use. Whatever I said was an excuse, for idleness, my own shortcomings, a reason to justify myself should I fail my exams. As for leaving at the end of the holidays that was nonsense. What he said was he'd leave when he found work. "Do you think I like staying here?" he said. "It's not much fun living with you". The point is I didn't know how to get rid of him. As the weeks went by I grew desperate. My work was suffering. The exams were approaching. I became moody and disagreeable. "I'm going to kick you out," I kept yelling at him. "I'm going to change the lock on the door, throw your things out of the window. I'm not your nurse maid. You can sleep in a doss house with drunks, dregs, drips — your own kind. I don't see why I should put up with you any more. I'm sick of the sight of you. You make me puke." He bore my ranting with equanimity. As long as I took no action he didn't care what I said. He let me feel I was using him as a scapegoat. I got the impression he was deliberately trying to make his prediction about my exams come true.

Then came an idea. I think it was towards the beginning of March. My exams were just over three months away. "Listen Bert, if I find you a job will you take it?" "What sort of job?" "Any job." He shook his head: "I don"t want to waste my abilities on something a moron could do." "Oh for Christ's sake," I screamed back, "you're good for nothing. I want to get rid of you. Take whatever you can get." This was the prelude to a filthy row. Not a fruitless one however, for out of it emerged the idea, his idea. He agreed to leave my place providing I found him somewhere else. Not any room, but one he didn't mind living in. I'd be responsible for the rent, but he'd contribute. Imagine: casting horoscopes; me to provide the clients. Minimum charge 10/- a time. The idea seemed so appealing I consented on the spot; anything to get rid of him. Don't get me wrong: I still needed him psychologically. I only wanted him out of my room, not out of my life. Next day I fixed him up with accommodation, £4 a week. (The cheapest he'd take.) Moving in was much the same as when he came to my place.

The first few weeks I had no difficulty finding him guinea pigs. I dug up relations, their friends, their friends' friends, Rita, Cyril, the boys and a host of others. Bert was casting horoscopes full time. At first I gave him the natal information as soon as I got it, but I quickly learnt my lesson, for he seemed to think once the rent was paid everything was his. We had a row about that. Finally we agreed to go fifty-fifty. But I wasn't taking any chances and thereafter rationed him. When he discovered what I was up to, which he did very shortly, he began hurling communist jargon at me: "Swindler; capitalist; imperialist; exploiter of the working classes." And more. He knew the Red phraseology off pat. I would protest: "Honestly Bert I've got nothing for you." "Why have you come then?" "I want to see how you do it." Here he would pause and look at me askew like a lizard frozen with uncertainty. "Do you really want to know?" he would ask eventually. "Sure I do. I wouldn't ask if I didn't". He would shake his head ponderously. "It's very complicated. It requires a lot of skill. It would take you years to master the subject." "You're a blinking marvel," I would answer pouring over his neck and gazing at the patterns and squiggles in front of him. Actually I liked watching Bert cast horoscopes; he concentrated like he was cutting his toe nails. It was a real pleasure to see him so immersed in a subject. "I hate it," he would tell me: "I only do it for the money." Bullshit of course.

By the end of the fourth week I was having serious problems. Clients were becoming few and far between. I was having to subsidize Bert more and more. He was costing me nearer seven pounds a week than four, not such a trivial sum that I could ignore. The crux of the matter was if I carried on spending as I had been doing I wouldn't be able to afford a summer holiday. And frankly I didn't want to miss it. I regretted my promise. I half wished Bert would get run over by a car, so he'd be at least hospitalized; anyway until my exams were over. But that was wishful thinking and I knew it. I struggled to find more clients. I put ads in the paper, posted others on bill boards, offered commissions, special rates, fast service. I don't know what I didn't try. No use, however. Clients diminished to a trickle and then nothing. Bang went all my prospects for a summer holiday. And it was all Bert's fault. Nor did he give me any sympathy. (The vitriol of my language he ignored.) All he was interested in was getting more clients. He couldn't believe I was having difficulty. "By now my name should be spreading. I expected people at my door step. I think you're holding something back on me. I doubt whether there's a person in England who can do a better reading than me." This was the sort of nonsense I had to put up with. And every day (sometimes two and three times) he came round to my place to see if I had work for him. It was as though my room was a call box. Then he would linger for hours, browsing through my books, eating my food, getting me to prepare him coffee or quite simply exercising his vocal chords. It was quite impossible to study when he was around. The truth was it didn't take much to pull me away from my work. Result: When it came to the exams I failed.

The next few days I felt terrible. I was shaken, so much so that I was ill with temperature. All my friends were on holiday: Sympathy, kindness, understanding were the last things I wanted. I didn't want to see anybody. Bert was different. Somehow I didn't view him as a human being. With him I felt I could let myself go. I paid him to stay with me and keep me supplied with provisions. For hours I would bemoan my fate: "I've got nothing to look forward to. My future is finished. I'll have to get a job I hate. Nine to five. Lousy pay. Uncongenial company. No prospects of promotion. Oh God it's too horrid to think of. " "You'll probably be a laborer," he grinned. At this I would flare up: "I don't know what you've got to be so happy about, you're the biggest washout I know. An all round failure. If I was in your shoes I'd go and throw myself in the Thames. I'm at least better than you are," "You don't have to be so sore about everything." (He still wore his computer grin.) "I checked your horoscope last night and you'll pass your exams next year." "I'm not taking any fucking exams next year," I exploded. "The examiners can go and stuff themselves. University is out, over and done with. I'll never take another shitty exam in my life. So much for your bloody predictions." "When you're in a different frame of mind your views will change". "And I suppose," I added bitingly, "that you're still going to be a roaring success, a genius, a woman charmer and all that other shit you've been giving me." "I have no reason to change my opinion," he replied like the oracle he thought he was. I snorted. The man was mad. What's more he was lucky to be mad. If I was mad I'd be out of my misery, for I'd be able to live in my own dream world, comfortable, secure, unaware. "I want to be nuts like you Bert," I whispered gently. Already I could see my reflection in the mirror and it was beginning to look like Bert.

When my sister, who lived in France, heard about my exam results she phoned me immediately. She was a practical woman and didn't waste much time with sympathy and post mortems. Right away she suggested I needed a change. The family had rented a chalet at Mégève for the summer. There was a spare room and no reason why I shouldn't use it. She brushed my excuses aside. The mountain air would do me good. In England I would only brood. I bowed to her judgment. A week later I flew to Lyons. Before leaving I told Bert I was through with him: He could become a boot-black in Piccadilly Circus for all I cared. "There's a shortage," I added nastily.

Ten days at Mégève and I felt much better. I wrote to the prof. at College and asked for a second chance. He'd already hinted I'd be taken back if I wanted. My letter was a formality. When, however, the affirmation came I felt much better. My immediate future became clear again. This put me at my ease and I started enjoying myself. And gradually the atmosphere of London began to fade. It was only about mid-September that I was jolted back to reality. News from Rita that her husband had died, leaving her penniless, without even a life insurance. There was a spare room in the flat. She would have to take in paying guests. She preferred somebody she knew to a stranger. Would I take the room? In the last paragraph she said Bert had gone to live in Portugal. That evening I cabled her my condolences and positive confirmation about the room.

I got back on the 29th. She greeted me cheerfully all in dark blue. I was surprised to see her so jolly considering the circumstances. The room was immaculate, even with flowers. I got the impression I was moving into a hotel bridal suite. A little later (as soon as it was diplomatically possible) I asked about Bert. Apparently he had gone to Portugal on account of a girl, "plump, short, a good deal older than him, but like him a washout". He had met Maria at Lyons Corner House (she didn't exactly know when) and subsequently had brought her round to the flat. "She's a woman like out of a Wagnerian opera. Loud, vulgar, very pretentious. She wants to marry an admiral. Bert isn't good enough for her. He gave her a scarf, but she likes only golden things, she says. That's real lower class, like the servants we had in Egypt. I suspect she was no more than a servant in Lisbon. She probably came to London to better herself, but when she saw she wasn't going to find what she wanted decided to go back. Bert was silly to follow her. But poor boy where will he find anything better? He's 33. He's ashamed in England without a job, girl or anything. At least in Portugal he'll have Maria. Though he'll be back very soon I'm sure." Then she told me I was well rid of him.

Next day she gave me a few scraps of dirty paper. "He gave me this, I forgot to tell you. It's crazy. I didn't understand a word." The bits of paper turned out to be an article from some astrological magazine. I read it carefully. It was very neat, typed with squiggles printed in black ink. There were lots of expressions I didn't understand. The article was boring, unreadable. "Was it published?" I asked handing it back. "Published." she exclaimed. "Who'd publish a thing like that?" When I replied it might mean something to astrologers she scowled, as though the proposition was ridiculous. So much for what she had to say about him on my return from my holidays. He had left no address and when I rung his mother to see if she knew where he was she accused me, incredible as it may seem, of corrupting him. "He was always a good boy. We did everything for him. Gave him corn flakes with bananas and cream every morning. Darned his socks. Sewed his buttons. Ran his bath. " I quietly hung up.

The months passed. I worked hard and in the summer

fooled the examiners. Again I spent the long holidays on the Continent. When I returned I found myself a room a block away from Rita's. (She had no vacancies at that particular time.) Then Bert, who, for eighteen months, hadn't shown a sign of life, was unexpectedly in town again. The first thing he did was to go and see Rita. One of her rooms was vacant and he promptly installed himself in it. I immediately went round to see him. Blow me he looked quite respectable. He wore a tweed jacket and his flannels had creases in the right places. His shoes were shining and about him there was an air of well-being. "You're looking fine," I told him. He replied he was moving up in the world. Portugal suited him. He wasn't a nobody like in England. "The English community in Lisbon detest me," he grinned. "I tell the natives the truth about this country. They don't believe me when I say the Government is riddled with corruption; that you can't get a decent job unless you've been to Eton or are related to the Prime Minister. You got the impression he said much more. In Lisbon he was giving English lessons. He'd written a book on English grammar, which was going to be published. He'd given one or two talks on teaching English to foreign students. He portrayed the scene very graphically: A battery of microphones in front of him; large audiences; the press scribbling away "hanging on to the pearls of wisdom that fell from my lips". I got the impression he had been speaking at the United Nations, of course the impression he wanted to convey. All said and done he seemed a reformed character. For the first time in my life I was envious of him.

The following day when I saw Rita she reassured me: "You don't believe all that rubbish he was telling you last night?" she said. "If you hadn't been there I would have told him, 'listen Mr. Bert you don't have to tell all those lies. We can see what sort of a person you are'. I was surprised to see you sitting, listening so intently, as though you were taking him seriously. He just wanted to impress you. And who's to verify what he says is true? You're not usually naive." I interrupted her: "What makes you think he's lying?" She made a rude noise, something like a snort. She said Bert hadn't changed at all. She even suggested his mother was still sending him money. As for his book, lessons, lectures, she dismissed them with a puff of her lips.

Bert stayed in London three weeks, supposedly to see about his book. He showed me a draft copy of it. I found it just as dull as the article on astrology he had written. I couldn't, with the best will in the world, imagine who would publish it. He divined my thoughts: "I'm having it published privately. It's always the way with anything good: The publishers are frightened to print it". That was that. I changed the subject. "What about your astrology, have you given that up?" "Not at all." He claimed he was just as interested in the subject as ever. He'd even written several more articles on it. Only trouble was the Anglo-Saxon countries didn't appreciate him — i.e. he'd only had rejections. "There's a hostility towards astrology in the English speaking countries. They think it superstition, non-scientific. If I wrote the sort of trash that gets published in the women's magazines I'd be all right." Then he elaborated at length (ideas I'd heard many times before) about establishing astrology as an exact science, reinstating astrologers as pillars of society, wielders of power. He cited several giants of the Middle-Ages. His knowledge of so much crap was prodigious. About his future he was just as optimistic. Glory burgeoned in front of him. He suspected his book would make him famous.

During the ensuing three years Bert returned to London twice. Nevertheless, he kept in touch with Rita. Now and again he dropped her a line on cheap note paper. She always showed me the letter. I would have to read it to her because she couldn't read his writing. Bert always gave the impression he was doing fine. More lectures. More students. Rave notices about his book, shortly to be translated into Portuguese. I half got the feeling he was a celebrity already. Rita, on the other hand, didn't believe a word he said. "He knows I show you his letters and wants to impress you." Anyway, about two years later, when he was back in London, I saw him again. This time Rita couldn't put him up. I was a little stunned by the change in him. He was wearing the same tweed jacket and flannel trousers he had worn two years earlier. The jacket was patched, the material fraying; it wasn't even clean. Then it looked as though he was wearing his gardening trousers. His shoes were cracked, caked with dirt and he had a big hole in one of the soles. His physical appearance was no better. He had a haggard look about him. He was pale; his face drooped; he seemed to have difficulty focusing his eyes. He hadn't had a haircut in months. He was growing a beard. He looked more like a tramp than an astrologer. At first he gave me the usual spiel — that he was doing fine, better than ever. Soon, however, I got to know the real situation. He'd been in trouble — over his visa, work permit, residential status. The authorities had at last caught up with him. He hadn't been allowed to be gainfully employed. Then he'd even got himself into trouble with the Church. He'd written an article (published at his expense I gather) proposing priests be disbanded and astrologers take their place — as advisors, counselors, moralists. In fact it was the article that first attracted the authorities' attention. In short Bert had been kicked out of Portugal.

This time Bert was in London several months. He told Rita and me he was writing frantic letters everywhere, He claimed he had powerful friends, who believed in the cause of freedom for Portugal and were antagonistic to the Church there. "I've started a revolution," he informed us coolly. He seemed to see himself as an operator from London, like Lenin was from Switzerland. His talk was very wild. He told us he was thinking of dropping Krush and Mao a line: "For their support". He expected no help from Britain or America. And of course the Catholic countries had a vested interest —

they'd do nothing for the cause of freedom. Bert had turned irrevocably against the Western world, which he described as decadent, hostile to genius, even talent and where no liberty existed. "And do you think it exists in the communist world?" I asked. He hedged: "The real hope for the world lies with the uncommitted nations. Nations like India." Then followed a long eulogy of India. "I may have to carry on my activities there if it gets too dangerous in England." "What activities?" He looked at me angrily. "The cause of justice and freedom." I smiled, but made no comment, neither did Rita. Then more twaddle. I got a kick out of listening to him. Sometimes I provoked him. Knowing him as I did the whole thing was ridiculous. He was the most harmless person I knew. To imagine him leading a revolutionary movement was as inconceivable as floating on air.

From Rita, with whom he seemed to open up more I got a further slant on his sex life, Maria apparently had been humiliating him. That's what he was really sore about. "She treated him as though he wasn't a man. She undressed in front of him, putting her legs up, undoing her suspenders, slipping down her knickers, wiggling her behind — trying to excite him, undressing like a stripper. Then when she saw he was moved, wanting her, she pushed him away, suggested he went to a prostitute. She even recommended one: A certain Rosie. Can you imagine the humiliation sending him to a professional? And then she wanted to know how much he paid her. She took a percentage, I bet you." Rita then gave me some technical details. He saw Rosie once a week. He placed the money on the table. She drew the blinds, then slowly undressed, giving him a little show. Everybody in the block thought he was giving her English lessons. "English lessons in the dark! But poor boy he's still attracted to Maria. He would marry her if he could, but she won't because she thinks he's beneath her. She's still looking for her admiral. Once he beat her up. I told him he was right. It's what any man would have done. Then you know what else she does, that domestic. She introduces him girls, acquaintances of hers. And in front of him tells them nasty things: How he doesn't know how to make love, would make a poor husband, is only a school teacher. According to Rita Bert's wild, revolutionary, anarchistic talk was only a sign of frustration. What he needed in his life was a real woman, not a servant.

A week or two later Bert started a school teaching job. He was sacked at the end of the third week. "They don't need brains to teach in a place like that. They need a sergeant major." To be sure he had then told the Head Master exactly what he thought of his school. Apparently the bloke had been offended. "Nobody likes the truth," explained Bert. The next job (don't ask me how he got it) was proof reading for *THE FORTUNE TELLER*, an astrological magazine. He was summarily dismissed after a fortnight. He assured me there was no justification. The editor had been prejudiced, envious of his brains, writing ability, skill as an astrologer. "All I did was make a few alterations in some of the texts. I wanted to improve them. I couldn't pass some of the nonsense they were giving me." He added as an afterthought: "I expect I was correcting most of the stuff he'd written. He was probably frightened I'd be made editor in his place." The only job he should have got but didn't was teaching English to foreign students. He tried. "All I have to do is show them the book I wrote and they turn me down flat." "Don't show it to them," I suggested. But Bert, according to him, was a man of principle: "It's foolish to let them persist in antiquated teaching methods when new and better ones are at hand." Bert, quite clearly, was unemployable, anyway in England. "You have to be dim and well connected," was his final verdict.

Why Bert wanted a job at all, and in England too was a different matter. Rita and I agreed. "He wants to show he can earn a living in England," she said: "Out there, there's no merit. Here, to be good means something." She paused and screwed up her nose: "I'm sure he'd really like to live here, but he's too proud. The only thing that kept him away so long was Maria. But he's not stupid. He knows what she's like. They were in a train together, traveling through France I think. *Wagons Lits.* He had the upper birth, she the lower. Next morning she told him she'd been very frightened because during the night the door opened and a ghost came in. When later he checked his wallet he discovered all his money had gone. 'You know Bert,' I told him: 'She was the ghost'. 'I think so,' he replied." But she now thought he had met his Waterloo and would settle in England. The very next day (after her prognostication) he came to say good-bye to me. He was returning to Portugal, he said. He would slip over the boarder like contraband. Once in the capital nobody would find him. He had been in England a little over three months. "He got a telegram from Maria," explained Rita. "He doesn't love her, but he knows she's all he'll get."

Three weeks later he was back in town again. He had been caught. In his inimitable way he told us what had happened. We had to imagine him crawling over the countryside, hiding behind shrubs, trees, rocks, dodging poison wood, insects, wild animals. The police had the dogs after him; searchlights swept the area; bullets zoomed here and there haphazardly. All the while he had been thirsty, hungry, soaked in perspiration, nauseous with fear and with a touch of diarrhoea. For one whole night he had gone without sleep. "Phew," he whistled as he proceeded with his story. We got the impression he had been tortured. Next morning he had given himself up. It had been too hot to run around the countryside like a little boy. Besides he hadn't liked the scenery, wanted a drink, a meal, a decent shit, lavatory paper provided. He then went on to tell us how he had been marched down the street, heavily guarded, soldiers on each side of him, the crowds thronging the pavements, gaping at him, mumbling, calling him the English spy. "I was taken to the local police station, through and out into the yard and ordered to stand still against the wall. "I thought they were going to shoot me." He paused for effect, smiled, made quite sure he held our attention, then went on: "As things turned out they only wanted to photograph me. They did it from all sides, as though they were taking polyphotos. There's now a huge file about me. I'm on their records as a dangerous criminal. Forbidden to enter Portugal under any pretext. To be fired upon at sight." He gave a sinister chuckle, as though it was an honor to be on a black list. He then told us about his night in jail. Damp, dreary, dirty. Lousy food. The toilet had been just a hole in the ground. A guard had stood over him, a rifle pointing at his head, every time he'd had a crap. The following day, he had been escorted, under armed guard to the Spanish border and given into custody to Franco's boys (khaki, rifle bearing midgets) and further escorted to the French border. "I'm not allowed in Spain either. I expect when the Pope gets to hear about me I'll be banned from Italy too." We asked what he intended to do? He replied as though the question was silly: "I'm going back to Portugal. I've written to Salazar explaining everything."

This time Bert didn't attempt to find work. He stayed with his parents, board and lodge provided. Most of the time, however, he was at Rita's. She didn't like him popping in and out, treating her place as though it was an office. Nor did her tenants, who complained about his using their toilet things, making a mess in the bathroom. "Tell him he mustn't come here," coaxed Rita. I told her she must do her own dirty work, forget about being kind hearted and generous. "Besides, what makes you think he'll listen to me? It's you who must speak to him." But she procrastinated. She hated turning anybody away. I did, however, attempt to do my share by trying to find out how long he intended to remain in the country. As usual he was vague. He wanted to return to Portugal, but somehow felt he had exhausted the country's possibilities and should move further afield. "The old countries are finished," he said.

"Hope lies with the new ones. Perhaps this time next year I'll be in one of them. There's no prejudice against genius in India. Maybe I'll go there." I looked him direct in the eyes and laughed loudly. "How bloody deluded can you get Bert? You're not far off 36, approaching middle age. Already your brain cells, what you of them, are decaying. Your whole body is atrophying. Yet you still think you're a genius. Grow up. You're no longer a little boy. Look at yourself in the mirror. You're a washout, a complete and utter failure. Why don't you admit it? At least have the courage to see yourself as you really are. You might even be happy. Forget all this crap about being a genius. You're not one and never was." Pause. Computer grin. I hadn't offended him in the least. "You like being nasty don't you? It gives your ego a boost." That's all he said. I couldn't contain myself and flared back: "There's no shattering your illusions, delusions. You'd rather die than admit you're like every body else. Less than everybody else." He walked away.

Surprisingly enough Bert was granted a pardon by the Portuguese Government and allowed to return. Only as a tourist however. When he left London for the first time in my life, I felt genuinely sorry for him. I took him to Victoria station and though he was as optimistic as usual, he suddenly struck me as being a very pathetic human being. Here he was deluding himself he was a genius. And because of it, unwanted, rejected, unappreciated. Poor man, I felt, that's all he had to cling to — an illusion as fragile as a pyramid of matches. Thank God he didn't listen to me. Standing on the platform speaking to him through the compartment window I had tears in my eyes. Bert had played an important part in my life. Now I was seeing him as he really was: a pitiable, struggling human being. Perhaps I was sorry for myself? What diabolical spirit had driven me to make a friend of such a man, a man who only stirred in me feelings of revulsion and contempt. Yet at the same time whom I needed. There he was then staring at me from the window his eyes goggling at me as they always did. He didn't look much older than when I first met him, but somehow he seemed different. It was as though something had snapped within him, a hope destroyed for ever. I sensed he knew now (inside I mean) that he was a washout, a failure and would never be otherwise. Rita was right. He pretended. The illusion was just something you showed people. A piece of self-advertisement, like you put a poster over a wall to cover the emptiness behind. That's how I felt standing on the platform.

Some weeks later Rita got a letter from Bert, the usual crap — short, a masterpiece of condensation. More students, lectures, astrological readings. (Naturally all clandestine.) An article published in New Delhi. Enclosed. He was still trying to negotiate the Portuguese translation for his book. His students were urging him to write another one. Money was coming in, but he had visa, dentist, Maria problems. "She's engaged to an ex-admiral! He's got tattoos all down his arms and chest. A common sailor if you ask me. His father, he went on to say, was dying. He sent me his regards. "He's a bloody fool," I said. "If they catch him this time they won't be so lenient." Rita shrugged: "I told him he was silly to go back. He should live in England among his own people. But he'll be back you see. He only went on account of Maria."

In the summer I went to Rimini for my holidays. Shortly after I arrived I got a long letter from Rita. All about Bert. He was back in London again, apparently on his way to India. "But he won't go," she wrote. No explanation. When I got back to London, however, he was already gone. But he didn't loose contact. He kept Rita informed. Every two or three months she got a letter from him, As far as we were concerned they didn't appear too different from those she had received from Portugal. The same tiny angular writing all on the one scrap of paper. He was doing fine. He liked India, the people, the atmosphere, specially the women. The big-wigs were beginning to take notice of him. His name was spreading. Articles published throughout the country. Examples enclosed, together with rave notices, letters about him, even a picture of him standing next to a Maharajah.

Then the next we knew Bert was he was getting married. This was some 19 months after leaving Europe. He told Rita all about it in another letter. It was going to be an excellent match, he wrote. The girl, he described, as young, beautiful, wealthy — the daughter of the Maharajah of Jahatispur. (Photographs were enclosed.) Next he went into reams of praise about the old man. You got the impression Bert was going to marry him, not the daughter. Apparently the Maharajah had everything: Immense power, colossal wealth, huge estates, life and death control over his subjects — including the privilege of sleeping with all the women he chose. "I'll probably be his heir." the letter informed us. Naturally Rita and I thought all this baloney. Who would want to marry Bert? And even if the marriage was arranged who'd want him for a son-in-law? Rita said the whole thing was a pack of lies. She still imagined he lived with the thieves, beggars, dregs, like in Portugal. She picked up the photographs and examined them. "She's pretty," she said judiciously. "She's very young. She looks only sixteen. But can you see Bert a husband? He wouldn't know what to do on the wedding night. I expect he bought the photographs. Who's to say they're genuine?" A day or two later, however, the whole business appeared in the British press. Allowing for the usual Bert exaggeration everything he had said was correct. Most of the blurb was about the Maharajah, but Bert was mentioned as an astrologer whose fame was spreading. We sent him a cable of congratulations.

From here on Bert's story is well known. You can read about it in any of the Indian libraries, or articles that have appeared in the British and American press. What neither Rita nor I knew (not until the articles first started coming out) was that India was the land of astrologers. There, they were respected. It was a noble profession. The highest and lowest listened to them. No decisions in private or public life were taken without them. Astrologers in India had much the same power that priests wielded in Europe during the middle ages. Bert, by going to India, had found his niche. But his first real break had come after his marriage when he was officially appointed adviser to the Maharajah. This had opened the door to him meeting the right people — in business, politics, science, other Maharajahs, V.I.P's of one description on another. Thereafter his rise to fame had been meteoric. The Maharajah of Jahatispur had always been a man of considerable influence, not only in his own territory, but throughout the country. After his daughter's wedding his power had grown still further and with it that of Bert. Bert had been riding on the shoulders of a giant and because he had been on the shoulders he had been able to see further than the giant. By the time Bert came to England he was the official astrologer of the Indian Government. The modern, progressive politicians perhaps didn't believe in astrology, but they had to tread cautiously because they were a minority and expedience prompted at least outward respect for these wise men. There had been no objection then when the Maharajah of Jahatispur had suggested in Lok Sabha (the Indian equivalent of the House of Commons) that Bert accompany him to England as part of a team to study British agriculture. He had argued that Bert would be invaluable in determining the astrological implications of scientific husbandry. It was when he came to London on this occasion, some four years after our last meeting, that I again saw him.

I paid him a visit at his suite at the Hilton. A big Indian man opened the door to me, but Bert, who was standing in the background, said it was all right and I was allowed in. "He's my body-guard," he explained apologetically; "I've got to be careful. You never know who might try and assassinate me." Bert glared at me through his powerful lenses. Next to him was his wife. I must admit I was bowled over, not just by him, but her as well. She was more than beautiful: She was exquisite: dark, with sensitive fine features, a perfect figure. The photographs didn't do her justice. But more than this, she was a delightful person, very feminine, gentle, loving. I was jealous. How did Bert get such a wife? So young too. At the time he must have been nearly forty. But perhaps that didn't matter, for in a sense he was beginning to look timeless. His hair was long. He wore a beard. About him there was an air of serenity, something I hadn't noticed before. Somehow he looked at peace with the world. In the course of the conversation he said he would spend the rest of his days in India and when be became old would be a saint. It struck me he was beginning to look like one already. He patted his wife on the rump and told her to run along. "But for time being," he grinned as soon as she was out of earshot, "a Rasputin kind of saint." I smiled. I suspected Bert had ample opportunity to gratify his sexual fantasies. Perhaps that's why he appeared so relaxed? All this was conjecture of course. I congratulated him on his success. He nodded as though the compliment was no more than his due. His manner was as I had always known it — ponderous, perceptive, positive of his destiny. Bert was still Bert.

There was still one thing I wanted to find out before I left. It had been troubling me. I had to have an answer, yet I didn't know how to frame the question. His marriage had made him famous. What I wanted to know was how in the hell had he persuaded the old man to give him his only child. The whole thing came bubbling out as I got up to say good-bye. "Listen Bertrand," I began nervously, "can you do me a favor? I don't mean to be rude. Don't answer if you don't want to." I paused and looked at him quizzically, but he remained silent (his eyes glaring through me) and I hurried on: "Well, I'll be blunt about it. I know you're not a person to hide behind a lot of verbiage. What I want to know is how did you acquire such a beautiful, wonderful wife? You're not exactly young, handsome yourself. And when you met her you didn't even have wealth

RITA

I STAND IN FRONT OF the mirror shaving. I use the old fashioned type of razor blades. For a moment I consider slitting my throat, doing the job properly and not just cutting myself as I usually do, The face that stares at me is long, thin, swarthy; the lips are full, the nose aquiline, the eyes a sad brown. But what particularly annoys me is my receding chin. I tried to cover it up with a beard once. No good of course. I'm still me nervy, indecisive. My natural inclination is to drift, wait for some sort of push to give me direction. I got to university that way. My parents did the pushing. (They died in a car smash last year.) Now I'm reading history, a subject I cordially detest. All my school teachers (may God rest their souls) said I was good at it. But that is not the end of my vacillation. Even the flat I'm living in is an accident. I was holidaying in Mégève recovering from an exam failure, when out of the blue I got this letter from Rita. She wanted to know if I would be her tenant? Cyril (her husband) had just died, she said, leaving her penniless, without even a life insurance. She would be forced to take in paying guests. She preferred me to a stranger. Of course I knew the room and liked it. I sensed too that I might get a break in the rent. Maybe I even thought I was doing Rita a good turn. No matter. I'm here, in her bathroom without any of the bother of having had to look for a flat when I returned to London. Now, after only three months, I am already asking myself whether I shouldn't move on.

Rita is a good sort. Egyptian. Jewess. Somewhere in her mid-fifties I suspect. Her age is top secret. (She keeps her passport at the bank specially so I won't find out how old she is.) She is as vain as hell, though I don't find her at all attractive. She is short and plump. Underneath her clothes she claims she has a beautiful figure! (Ha. Ha. Who is she kidding?) Her face is long with numerous chins, baggy cheeks and piles of fair hair which she does up in a bun. When she goes out, rain or shine, she plonks a ridiculous hat on her head. Her dresses, incidentally, are always dark with hem lines going well below the knees. But Rita has a nice smile and warm, tender brown eyes. Everybody likes her. The family had met Cyril and Rita Nessim years ago when visiting Cairo and somehow the link had continued. When I came to London to study it was only natural (Ma's suggestion) that I should drop in and see them.

There is a knock on the door.

"What is it?" I ask.

"How long are you going to be?"

"For God's sake, Rita. leave me in peace."

"What time do you want your breakfast?"

"I'll be ready in fifteen minutes."

Pause. Then she asks me what my sister has said about her the night before. I pretend not to hear. She repeats the question. "I'll be out of the bathroom in five minutes," I answer.

My thoughts shift to the previous evening, My sister has visited the flat. Tall, slender, approaching thirty, she is a very elegant woman. She lives in Geneva, but furnishes her wardrobe mostly in Paris. The night before she had been wearing a bright green dress, high neck line and with a lapel going over to one shoulder. I too had preened myself for the occasion. (My sister is always very critical about the way I dress.) I had put on my best suit, single breasted, dark grey with thin blue streaks. My tie was striped red and black on a white shirt. Rita said I looked stunning. My sister said nothing at all. Rita wore her usual dark blue dress, probably something our grandmothers would have worn. But she had perfumed herself and in the morning had been to the hairdresser. Her hair looked as though it had been plonked on her head in the same sort of way she usually puts her hat on. After the three of us had had dinner at the local steak house I took my sister back to her hotel in a taxi. During the ride she gave me her verdict. The room is all right, well furnished, large, bright. No criticism there. Rita, if she has met before in Egypt, she doesn't recall. Then she goes on, no mincing of words:

"She's absolutely crazy over you poor woman! I understand why you see each other perfectly. You need to feel superior, boss people, feel yourself master of every situation. This Mrs whatever-her-name-is, probably sees you as a son. No doubt she regrets not having had one herself. You came into her life just at the right moment. You filled the vacuum left by the death of her husband. I know you tell me she didn't love him, but she's the sort of woman who has to love somebody. I expect she really couldn't live without her husband. When you came along you somehow took his place as well as the son she'd never had and wished she had. That's why poor soul she's prepared to stick anything from you. I'm sure she feels very empty inside. She's probably very lonely. She knows if she wants to keep you it'll be only on your terms. You play a cat and mouse game with her. But if you want my opinion she's not at all good for you. A normal girl wouldn't tolerate that sort of thing. As long as she's around I can't see you getting married. She wouldn't want you to get married of course; and you know how much I'd like you to. I'm sure you'd loosen up a bit and be ever so much more pleasant. You know I say all this for your own good, because I love you."

I had nothing to say to that. How, in less than a couple of hours she had managed to sense the peculiarity of our relationship beats me. It is true that Rita was particularly jittery, fussing over this and that, first at the flat and then at the restaurant. She kept apologizing about not being able to offer us anything better than tea and biscuits. Then excusing herself that the biscuits were a bit stale, broken, not the best quality. Sorry that the flat wasn't cleaner, tidier, but that the daily had neglected to come. In the restaurant she kept chopping and changing her mind about her order, where she wanted to sit (there was a draft), whether she should keep her coat on or take it off. Then she talked. God how she talked. She didn't stop. She was trying to be sweet, impress; but it was painful. My sister sat sedate, polite, smiling: she said very little. On one or two occasions I snapped. I couldn't help myself. When I am alone with Rita and she starts gabbling away I tell her bluntly to shut up. If she doesn't I yell or even insult her. (My sister obviously noticed my little outbursts. Also the way Rita took them). All this is very bad for me I know. That's one of the reasons I'm thinking of moving. Rita brings out the worst in me. I hate myself when I speak to her as I do. Yet I persist. I go into my room and dress.

A few minutes later Rita bounces in with breakfast. "I have made you a meal fit for a king," she beams as she puts a mess of scrambled eggs on the table.

You forgot to sew my shirt button on," I tell her.

"I looked. There wasn't one missing."

"You didn't look very well." I show her one of the cuffs on a sleeve.

"I'll do it now." She bustles out of the room.

"WAIT!" I cry. She stops at the door. "The eggs are cold."

"You can't expect me to keep them hot if you don't tell me exactly what time you want breakfast."

"Warm them up please."

She leaves the room. I sip my tea. I really must get out of this nut house, I say to myself. But then another part of me protests. The room is fine; the price is right: where else will I find complete maid service for what I am paying? But Rita is more than a maid. She boosts my ego, She tells me all sorts of wonderful things about myself. She listens to my ravings over this and that. From her I am learning about women. Don't get me wrong, there's no sex between us. Physically she leaves me cold. She keeps telling me what I need is a little love. The implication being she can give it to me. "What is the difference between LOVE and FUCK?" I have asked her a number of times. "They're both four letter words aren't they?" "There's a world of difference," she laughs. "Though if you F— with the right girl you might learn to love." (Rita can never say FUCK.) She returns with the eggs, She is looking as pleased as a baby that has just been tickled.

"Rita," I tell her pompously. "I have decided to quit. This is my formal notice."

Her face droops. She looks at me incredulously: "What: just because the eggs weren't hot?"

"Oh don't be silly."

"Why then?... Ah yes, I know. Your sister told you to leave." When I don't reply she goes on: "If it was genuinely your decision I wouldn't mind. But I don't like you being influenced by everybody. You can tell your dear sister that I am not harming her darling brother and if it wasn't for me you would be in a very bad state."

"Rubbish, Rita. You're deluding yourself. You've been very kind to me. Rather you've tried to be. But put it into your head that spiritually you've done nothing for me."

"You'll only understand later, when it'll be too late and I'll be pushing up daisies; but tell me what did your sister say about me?"

"Nothing nice."

"I didn't expect it. A woman like that can't possibly understand a woman like me."

"Is there anything to understand?" I grin.

She laughs: "You don't know how much good I'm doing for you."

"You do a lot for me Rita, I don't deny it: you keep my room clean and tidy, cook for me, mend my clothes, do a hundred little jobs about the flat. I'm most grateful."

She guffaws. "A maid could do all those things. I do much more than that."

"What for instance?"

"Don't you see? I want you to be yourself, natural. Who else do you speak to like you speak to me?"

"Yes, Rita, I agree, you bring out the worst in me."

She gives a little shrug of despair, turns her eyes toward the ceiling. "You still haven't told me what your sister said. It must have been really bad to sway you so."

"She didn't say anything that you or I don't already know."

"If that's the case there's no harm in repeating what she said."

"Okay, you've asked for it. " And for the next few minutes I outline what my sister said. I give it to her straight. I don't spare her at all. "You see she too thinks you bring out the worst in me," I conclude.

"Madam, your dear sister understands me even less than I thought. And as for understanding you she doesn't even begin to understand you. You can tell the dear woman that I don't love her brother at all in the way she thinks."

"How do you love me, Rita?"

"I don't love you at all. How could I love a monster like you? I like you very much. I'm very fond of you. But that's only because I see your soul, underneath your facade."

"You just told me you wanted me to be myself. Being a monster is being myself. How do you reconcile that with what you just said?"

She flicks her hands impatiently. "Cut the philosophy. Just be natural, that's all I ask of you," Then she goes on philosophically: "My father always said there are two sides to man: the angel and the devil. I see the angel in you, but it doesn't mean I'm unaware of the devil."

"Okay, Rita, enough cackle. I've got work to do."

She moves towards the door then stops. "You were joking when you gave me notice weren't you?"

"Not at all. I'll be leaving you a week tomorrow"

"Stay, I can do so much good for you."

"My decision is irrevocable."

"You do let yourself be influenced don't you? It's very bad for you. You must learn to make your own decisions."

I jump up from the table. She has touched a sore spot. I feel my adrenaline flowing. I stride threateningly towards her. I just want to frighten her. "Go," I yell "before I lose my temper. Put it into your head that my sister has nothing to do with my leaving you. I've been meaning to leave you for ages. I want you out of my life."

She looks at me sympathetically. Her eyes are reaching out to me. My outburst hasn't frightened her in the least. She comes back into the room."What have I done to you that I deserve you say that?"

"Go," I scream. "Otherwise I don't hold myself responsible for my actions." She doesn't budge. We are a couple of feet away. I want to kick her or hit her. But I do nothing. Just glare. Her eyes are radiating warmth and love. I lick my lips, my face twitches; I can feel the sweat in the palms of my hands. I control my emotion and speak softly, letting the vitriol of my feelings come out in words: "Listen, Rita, I want to make it clear to you once and for all, that I want you out of my life because you are a pain in the ass. You pester me, prevent me from working, talk too such and as for your advice … I shit on that … I don't see you at all how you see yourself. To me you're a stupid neurotic woman chasing a younger man. What you want from me is a fuck. But I'm not going to give you one. Never. Do you understand? I find you repulsive. You don't attract me at all. If it's sex you want I suggest you go elsewhere. But if you want my candid opinion I think you'll have to pay for it."

By now I am beaming, The tirade has done me good. Rita has registered no emotion. (She has heard it all before.) As she leaves the room I am overwhelmed by a flood of feeling. Tears are running down my cheeks. I want to apologize. But another part of me holds me back. "You are being weak," a voice within says. I do nothing. I stand riveted.

A week later I move to a bedsitter five minutes down the road. Also spacious and bright, but a good deal more expensive. The final week with Rita has been turbulent: bickering, rows, shouts. On one occasion I actually hit her, though I was sorry afterwards. I am pleased with my decision to leave her. The last thing I tell her is I never want to see her again, nor hear from her.

Two days later she has me on the phone. "Peter," she cries, "Something terrible has happened."

"WHAT?" I shriek unpleasantly.

"One of my relations has died and I have to go to the funeral and I don't like going to funerals and I've got nothing to wear."

I say a few sympathetic words.

"Come with me," she begs.

"WHAT!"

"I told my relations you'd take me to the funeral in your car."

"You've got a nerve Rita."

"Won't you do it then?… Please."

"I suppose I can hardly refuse… when is the funeral?"

"Tomorrow." She gives me particulars and I arrange to pick her up at the appointed time.

She is ready waiting for me when I pass with the car. Mourning suits her. Somehow, black goes with her complexion.

She is wearing no make-up. A black scarf is wrapped over her head and ears. Her appearance is solemn. She looks like a Muslim woman without a veil. As soon as she gets in the car she begins her chatter. This time about the dead relation. She was a dear soul, very rich, but money had not spoilt her. She adored Rita.

"Anyway she couldn't have been very generous," I say.

"She always did her best for me," Rita replies.

Pause. She then wants to know what I think of her dress? She has just bought it. I look at it. It looks exactly like her blue dress except it's black. It is too long, without shape, old fashioned.

"I don't understand," I falter. "Didn't you have one from your husband's funeral?"

She hesitates: "I just couldn't go to his funeral," she answers at length.

"I expect all this is bringing back memories."

She doesn't reply, but I can see there are tears in her eyes.

Presently we get to the cemetery: rows and rows of neatly arranged tombstones, some with flowers, some without; here and there a more impressive tomb, a little monument, a mausoleum. As we walk on the path the pebbles crunch under our feet. Mitzi, Tutzi, Isaac, Solomon, names Rita has often mentioned — they are all there. There are about two dozen people in all, including children. Everybody is in black, solemn, silent, waiting for the interment to begin. We are standing round a grave. The coffin is large, long, in very dark wood. A man starts spouting prayers. I find the whole scene depressing. (This is the first funeral I have been to since my parents died.) The ceremony seems to go on and on. Women are wiping their eyes with handkerchiefs. There is a lot of sniffling, stifling of sobs and now and again an extra loud sob.

Eventually the whole business is over, We are walking, grim, like a procession of monks and nuns, towards the exit of the cemetery. I am on my own. I am trying to feel part of the group, but I don't. Rita's relations don't seem too bad I think. (She has always described them as dull, staid, boring.) They are now jabbering in subdued tones. Are they speaking Arabic or Yiddish? I don't know. I switch to my own thoughts. Why have I let Rita come back into my life? What am I doing at this funeral? Am I still attracted to Rita? Love, hate? Maybe I should go to an analyst? I am interrupted from my introspection by a tall, pale, middle-aged woman. Her voice has a trace of an accent.

"You're Peter aren't you? …we've heard a lot about you."

"Nothing bad I hope."

"Not at all. Very complimentary." She hesitates, smiles thinly: "You know Mrs. Nessim is very fond of you. You're like a son to her… You know…" She breaks off in the middle of her sentence. "I don't know if I should tell you? I don't know what Rita has told you?"

"What about?"

"Her son."

"Her son?" I repeat incredulously. "I didn't know she had one."

"What! Hasn't she told you?"

"No. She's told me nothing of the kind."

"Oh! Then perhaps I'd better not say anything."

Here I am at a loss for words. I am dying to know more. I want her to keep talking, but I don't know how to encourage her. In the mean time the opportunity is lost, for a short, fat, round faced man has joined us. He makes a facetious remark. He strikes me as being a bore. A few minutes later I am in the car on my way home. Rita has remained with her relations. I too was asked back to one of their homes, but refused saying I had a paper to prepare. I sort of felt, with the family around, I wouldn't get very much out of Rita. I was itching to know about her son. All the way home I keep turning the thing over in my mind. "Fancy Rita hiding that from me?" What I can't get over is she has kept a secret and she didn't seem to be the sort of woman who could. It strikes me there is a lot about Rita I don't know. She has always told me I don't understand her. I'm beginning to think she may be right.

That evening after dinner (though it is raining) I drop in at Rita's place. She isn't home and she later tells me she spent the night at her relations. Next day, round about lunch time, she still isn't back and it isn't until that evening that I finally get hold of her.

She is still in black, but when she sees me she beams: "What do I owe the honor of this visit?" she wants to know.

"Can I come in?"

I follow her into the sitting room, sparsely furnished with sofa, two easy chairs, dining table with four chairs, blue carpet and drapes.

"Why didn't you tell me you had a son?" I immediately blurt out.

"Who told you?"

"One of your female relations at the funeral."

"She shouldn't have done. Who was it?... oh I know." Then she rattles away excitedly. Words pour from her mouth like hot air from a punctured tire. Comment, criticism, abuse; explanations and rationalizations. It all amounts to a lot of horse shit. No gems in this manure.

I stamp my foot impatiently. "For God's sake Rita stop driveling. Tell me about your son."

She gives me a hard look. There is a moment's silence. I fiddle with my fingers nervously. When she replies I am a little staggered. "I haven't got a son," she says.

What!"

"He's not like me at all. There's nothing of me in him. He's like his father."

"I don't get you Rita. Explain yourself. Have you a son or haven't you?"

She gabbles away as though I hadn't spoken: "In seven

months he came. He was a lovely baby. The doctor said he'd never seen such a wonderful baby. He was very big for seven months. He hurt a lot. I'm rather small you know. You may think that because I'm a little on the fat side I'm big, but down there I'm small. He was a wonderful child. If I'd brought him up he'd have been quite different. But nobody let me get near him. I did my best, but Cyril was jealous every time I gave Michael any attention. He wanted all the attention himself. I know Michael would have been all right if I'd had him. But they wouldn't let me. He's like his father. He not like me..."

Again I interrupt: "I don't understand Rita. Why couldn't you bring up your son?"

"They wouldn't let me."

"Who's they?"

"They." She is looking a little bewildered.

Pause. I am beginning to understand what she is getting at. "What I think you mean is that you did bring your son up, but because you made a mess of it, like you do everything else, it isn't your fault and others are to blame."

Her eyes flash. She is very indignant. She says I don't understand anything. Perhaps when I have children I will. She isn't to blame at all for what happened to her son.

"What happened to him?" I ask.

"He's away."

"Thanks for the precision. Away where?"

"Just away."

"In a loony bin," I suggest.

She laughs: "Nobody in my family is mad. We're all of good healthy stock."

"Excluding yourself of course," I slip in with a mischievous grin.

"I'm the healthiest of the lot. I've never been sick in my life."

"You mean physically?"

She makes a rude noise. "Fortunately I don't believe a word you say."

"Well, getting back to the point. If your son isn't in a loony bin where is he?"

"He'll be going to a hospital shortly."

"What sort of hospital?"

"A very nice hospital."

"Oh for God's sake Rita stop being so evasive. Is the hospital a mental institution?"

"Some of the patients may be mentally disturbed," she answers.

I grunt, scowl , scratch the back of my head thoughtfully. Rita in staring at me vacantly with wide brown eyes. I sense she is nervous. "You say your son is going to this hospital implying he isn't there already. Where is he now?"

She hesitates then tells me: "In a home for naughty boys."

"You mean Borstal."

"What is Borstal?"

"The unexpurgated version of a home for naughty boys." Then I ask her why she hasn't told me about Michael before?

"He's not my son.'"

"You mean you disown him because he didn't conform to the image you wanted of him?

"There's a lot you don't know," she answers irritably.

"What?"

"A lot, I don't tell you everything. There are millions of things I could tell you, but you never give me a chance. You always tell me to shut up."

"You only give me advice and that's boring. You never tell me anything interesting."

"You never let me."

"All right, I never let you. But tell me, don't you ever go and see your son or write to him?"

"No. It wouldn't be good for him to see or hear from me.

The doctors say that memories of the past only upset him. He must get used to living without me now. We did all we could for him and he ruined us.

"Ruined you? What do you mean?"

"He spent all our money. My money, for my husband didn't have any."

"You didn't tell me Cyril married for money."

She gives a forced laugh. Then she tells me they spent a fortune on Michael's education, sending him to the best schools, giving him private tuition, letting him learn the piano. Then they spent even more on doctors and analysts. And more still paying his gambling debts, the bills he used to run up here and there and the fines he had to pay in court. "We did everything for him."

There is a pause. Rita has turned away from me. I sense the conversation is upsetting her. She fidgets with her fingers, dress, hair. She wants to know if I want tea or coffee, perhaps something to eat.

"Nothing thanks Rita. I have to go."

She turns and faces me, eyes watery with tears. "Stay," she begs.

I take her in my arms, kiss her on the forehead, hold her for a little while. I can feel her breathing and heart throb against me. Her head is on my shoulder.

Then abruptly she pulls away. "Why don't you spend the night here. It's cold outside. You can sleep in my bed and I'll sleep on the sofa."

"No dice Rita."

"If you want to bring a woman up you can," she adds enthusiastically. "I'll hide in the kitchen. Nobody will know I'm here. I just want to know what sort of women you like." Then a little coyly, her voice barely above a whisper, a hand groping between my legs, she suggests she wouldn't mind seeing me perform.

I laugh disengaging myself. "I must go Rita. It's getting

late." I give her a goodnight peck. She tries to hold me tight and for a few moments I let her, then I pull away. "I'm going. Goodnight."

"Can I come and see you in the morning?"

"No."

"Wouldn't you like to see a photograph of Michael?"

"Very well. Show it to me quickly."

"The photographs are at the bank with my passport. If you let me come round to your place tomorrow I'll bring them then."

I know what that means, but I can't resist the temptation. Foolishly I agree, but I make it clear that she will only be able to stay a short time. "As soon as I've seen the photographs out you go. No procrastination, understand."

A few minutes later I am walking along the wet glistening pavement back to my bedsitter. Though it is late the streets are still crowded. The night shift is on the prowl: dregs, drips, drunks, pimps, prostitutes and their patrons. Now and again you see a cop. I am sprayed by a shower of water as a cab hurtles through a puddle. Silently I curse. I should watch where I am going instead of looking at the girls. Half an hour later I am in bed.

Next day Rita brings an album of photographs. Pictures of Michael nude kicking, smiling on a blanket; sitting stern, struggling on the potty; in his mother's arms, in his father's arms, riding a donkey, playing in a sand pit. Simply hundreds of snapshots. But I'm not particularly interested in the earlier ones. To me all babies look alike. What I want to know is what Michael looks like now. The most recent photographs are three years old. They are taken professionally, therefore good. Michael was thinking of becoming a film star. There are head and shoulder shots, full length, smartly dressed, casual and in bathing trunks. His hair is fair, face round and jolly, retroussé nose, the eyes are dark and resemble Rita's. In fact in many respects the youth has a lot of Rita. The thick chin, large cheeks, sensual lips. I tell Rita what I think. She says he looks like his father, that he has nothing of her. I don't argue. Eventually I hand her back the album, thank her for bringing it along and tell her to go.

"What! You're not going to make me go just like that," she protests.

I nod. "It's what I said last night."

But she finds something to do: washing up, making my bed, tidying and cleaning the room. I hate these chores so I let her do them. That unfortunately was the beginning. Thereafter she became a sort of *au pair*. At first she came twice a week, but then she said it would be less work for her if she came more often. So she came more often and very soon she was popping in and out (she had a spare key) precisely when she felt like it. It wasn't very different from living with her in the flat. It was back to old times: rows, insults, misunderstandings. I berated myself for my weakness. Yet I liked her around the place, not only for what she did in the room, but also because I was lonely and to some extent she kept my spirits up. Quarreling is not boring, though I hate it. I would tell Rita continually that I wanted her out of my life; then the next thing I would be doing is asking her to come round and do some mending for me. My moods oscillated like a yo-yo. Sometimes I wished she would be ill, or get run over, anything to stop her coming round. At other times I would stand watching at the window waiting for her to arrive. I just somehow couldn't get her out of my system. And so our relationship continued, pretty much the same as in past.

I just kept staring at the paper. Nothing would come. I was paralyzed. I had written number at the top right hand corner of the page. The other students were busy scribbling away. The only sounds were the scratching of pens or the occasional cough. Why hadn't I anything to say? I knew what I had to write, yet all I could feel was a vague emptiness, a weakness in the pit of my stomach; my legs were twitching. I sense that my father is pouring over my shoulder, breathing heavily, saying nothing, but somehow disapproving, communicating what a disappointment I was to him: "it's the result that counts." I can hear the words— "only the result. The result. The result." The phone is ringing. "What's the use of trying if you don't get the result you want? Result. Do you understand?" The phone continues to ring. I mustn't answer. Dring…Rrr.ing … Rrrr. ing…

The phone is actually ringing and when I answer it is Rita on the other end. "Peter, I've been trying to get hold of you for ages. I tried all yesterday afternoon and evening. Where were you? Something has happened very important. Can I see you immediately?"

"God Rita you gave me a start. I was in the middle of a nightmare. I dreamt I failed my exams. I must have drunk a little too much last night. What time is it?"

"Nearly 11 o'clock. I'm sorry I woke you. You're not usually asleep this late. Please can I come and see you. Now. Immediately. It's very important."

"Can't you tell me on the phone?"

"I'd prefer to see you."

"Is this a trick just to come here?."

"No, no. I promise you. I swear on my father's head, something very important has happened. Will you let me in if I come?"

I grunted "all right."

Sunday morning. The morning after the night before. I'd been to a party and eaten too much, drank too much, stayed too late. I went into the bathroom and sluiced my face with cold water. My eyes are bloodshot, the skin is red under the whites, there are dark rings underneath. I have a nasty taste in my mouth. I push my tongue out. It is grey with streaks of white. I brush my teeth, gargle, put Optrex in my eyes. I fill the kettle with water, put it on my little electric heater, then go back to my room and bury myself under the sheets.

By the time Rita arrives (she took longer than I thought she would) I have had some coffee and feel much better. I am in my dressing gown sitting at the table.

"Peter," she cries, boiling over with excitement as soon as she sees me. "You know that old woman who died, my relation whose funeral you went to a few weeks ago. Well, she's left me all her money."

I give a little start. "I'm delighted Rita," I reply unenthusiastically, as though I was a courteous bureaucrat thanking a customer for allowing me to serve him.

"I could get a much larger flat now. You could have two rooms to yourself, private bathroom too. You wouldn't have to pay a penny. And I'd have a maid to do your room, cook, do anything you want."

"What are you talking about Rita?"

"If I got a nicer place wouldn't you come back to me? I wouldn't disturb you I promise."

"You must be out of your mind woman. I wouldn't live with you for anything under the sun. You know what I think of you."

"You don't say what you mean. You like me very much, but you won't admit it to yourself I don't know why. Everything you say about me is exactly the reverse."

I make a rude noise. I am staring at Rita slightly amused. She is standing in the middle of the room exactly like when she first came in. She in still wearing her hat and coat, both dark blue with stockings to match and black shoes. She looks a bit like fortune teller I had once consulted in Soho up some rickety old stairs just off Piccadilly. I had difficulty believing she is real.

"I know you don't like England very much," she is saying. "Neither do I. I much prefer the sunshine, open spaces, good fresh air. If you like we could go and live abroad, somewhere quiet, where nobody knows where we are and who we are. You wouldn't have to work or do anything you don't want. I've got enough money for both of us. I'd make you very happy. You could even have all the girls you want. I wouldn't be jealous. You'd be absolutely free. All I want is your happiness."

"Why don't you take your hat and coat off Rita and sit down. Here let me help you." And I suit action to word. "I don't think you're too well this morning. Your good news has deranged your thinking a little."

She brushes me aside and takes her own things off. Underneath she is wearing the same old blue dress. One of the stockings has a ladder. She remains standing. "My thinking is perfectly clear," she says with composure. "I know what I'm saying and I'm not joking. I've started trying to help you and I want to finish the job. I don't like unfinished work."

"Rita," I say gently, a smile on my face. "You tell me you've got plenty of money now. I believe you, And I even think, if money is no object, you'll find yourself a boy friend. But don't put me on your list. Count me out."

"You don't know what you're saying," she retorts. "You're talking upside down again. I don't want a boy friend. I want you. Do you think I'd make such an offer to just anybody?"

"Rita. Put it into your head I'm not going to be your boy friend. Nor am I going to live with you again. Once is enough. More than enough."

"We could go and live on a little West Indian Island."

"Why a West Indian Island?" I ask tongue in cheek. I have decided to play her game.

"I want to be away from everybody."

"I would have thought you'd want to show off now you've got money. You're a very vain sort of woman."

"I don't want anybody to know I've got money."

"Why Rita? Are you frightened you might have to give some away?"

"That's not it at all," she protests indignantly.

"Why then?"

"Because."

"I must admit you're very explicit when you want to be."

"I can't tell you."

"Another one of your secrets?"

She smiles but doesn't reply. She prepares me eggs on toast for brunch, gives me a fruit salad for dessert. When I am again sipping more coffee she returns to her main point. What harm is there if I go away and live with her, she wants to know? Sunshine, girls, freedom, luxury, idleness. She feeds me with her bait as though I was some kind of fish. Then, when I am still unmoved she expands, highlighting the publicity like a stubborn saleswoman: "You would meet all sorts of interesting people; you would be seeing new places; we could go for cruises; we could even afford to rent a yacht..."

"Rita, you're a scream," I laugh as I cut her short. "If I told anybody about you they wouldn't believe me."

"If you won't come away with me I'll have to stay in England and I don't want to."

"I'm not forcing you to stay here Rita. You can go where the hell you like. I don't care a damn."

"Who would look after you if I didn't?"

I snort. I tell her I am expecting people and she must go. It isn't true, but that is the quickest way to get rid of her. Eventually she reluctantly leaves. "If you want me I'm at the flat," she says.

The days and weeks that follow I see Rita quite a lot. I notice a change in her. I don't only mean she has bought herself a few new clothes, gone to the hairdresser more often, that sort of thing. The change is more subtle. She was always nervous, but now she appears even more so. Her talk is a constant babble. Even when I listen she doesn't make much sense. Then she started doing things she never did before like a little drinking on the side when she was alone at her place, or when she was with me helping herself to some of my brandy or whisky, sometimes even without my permission. She started smoking again, a habit she had given up years ago. Then she had kicked her tenant out. And the flat, instead of being neat and tidy as it had always been, became neglected. Even her clothes changed. Instead of being immaculate in her 1920 outfit of dowdy dark dresses she took to wearing bright colored dresses, length well above the knees, light stockings (or no stockings if it was warm),high heeled fancy shoes, sassy hats. She was really quite a sight. Was she trying to seduce me? Perhaps. It struck me she might be heading for the same establishment as her son.

Nor did she give up urging me to leave the country with her. Every time I saw her she dangled the same old bait under my nose. I would laugh and the more I laughed the more she persisted, and the next time I would see her she would be dressed even more unbecomingly. At first I didn't take all this too seriously, but gradually it dawned on me that Rita was sick, or certainly very emotionally disturbed. Initially I think I was under the impression that once the excitement of her inheritance had worn off she would revert back to her old self. Nothing of the kind however. Time only made things worse. She gave me the impression that she was expecting something to happen, something very sinister and we simply had to be away before a certain deadline. I even thought that perhaps Rita had got herself into trouble with the law. I questioned her about the possibility but she denied it emphatically. Then it struck me something had happened to her son or perhaps she felt guilty about the whole business.

"Is your son all right?" I asked.

"I don't know. We don't communicate."

"Why don't you take him out of the dump he's in and put him somewhere better. You can afford it now."

She is offended. She says she has done her best for him. "On that score I have nothing to reproach myself. He has seen all the best doctors. The hospital he is at now looks after him very well. They understand his case. It is better that we do not communicate. I would love to see him, but the doctors tell me it is better I don't. Seeing me would bring back memories and that would hurt him. I love him very much. Fate has dealt us a very cruel blow."

"You may be right," I reply. "But I still don't understand what's come over you in the last few weeks. You've been very nervous; you've been drinking too much; you've started smoking again; then look at yourself. You're simply not you, or anyway your old self."

"It's because you won't come away with me."

"Of course I won't come away with you. I've told you a thousand times the proposition is absurd. But that's no reason why you should be so nervous."

"If you don't come away with me you won't see me so often."

"Hallelulah."

"I'm not joking. I mean it. From tomorrow you'll see much less of me. And you mustn't just pop round to my place when you feel like it. If you do I won't receive you."

There is something in her tone which makes me feel she means what she says. She is looking at me a little distantly. Her eyes are very bright, unnaturally so as though she was on dope. I half wonder if she isn't drunk.

"Do you know what you're saying Rita?"

"Of course I know what I'm saying."

"What is it then? Why won't you tell me?"

No answer.

"I want to know the truth. You owe it to me."

"I owe you nothing," she snaps. "You were right. I am a stupid neurotic woman."

"What has made you see the light?" I can't resist saying, a gentle supercilious smile about my lips.

"You. You have. You have taught me a lot. For that I thank you very much."

"What have I taught you?"

"You have taught me to appreciate my friends, my real friends. My relations may be a bit on the dull side, but they are at least kind. They have tried to help me within their means. And Cyril too. He may have used me, been abrupt sometimes; but there were many extenuating circumstances in his case. It wasn't easy for a man of his age to come and start a new life in a foreign country. He hated to see me slaving around the house, cooking, cleaning, queuing in the shops when in Egypt we had five servants. Then your sister isn't the only one to get her dresses in Paris. At one time all my dresses were *Balmain, Dior, Chanel*. I was one of the smartest women in Cairo. The change wasn't easy for us. I was stronger than Cyril. When you used to come around he always used to put on a front, pretend the business was prospering, that we still had money, that everything was fine. But you don't know what we went through on account of Michael. That was the most bitter blow of the lot. Leaving Egypt we could get over. Losing our money. Well, that wasn't the end of the world. But our own flesh and blood…"

She turns away and begins crying in loud semi-hysterical sobs. She takes out a handkerchief from her sleeve and begins dabbing her eyes. I take her by the shoulders and try to reassure her. Gently I caress her, kiss her on the back of the neck, stroke her hair. She doesn't respond and wiping her eyes, chokes back her sobs,

"I'm sorry Rita. I know how you feel. I wish I could do something."

"You have destroyed me," she whimpers. "I thought I was strong, But you have obliterated me, annihilated me, made me into a doormat."

"How so Rita? I don't understand."

She goes over to a cupboard and opens the door. Inside

there is a full length mirror. She points to herself, her hand trembling."Look. Look. Is that me?"

Five foot two; bright red dress, almost mini; low neck line, breasts large, heavy, trying to spill out; drooping gold chain belt; saucy mauve berry with pom pom on the top; black crochet-like stocking practically bursting around her thick thighs: Rita's garb makes her look like a caricature of a chorus girl and her make-up that of a clown: the cheeks are heavily rouged, thick with layers of powder; her lips sticky with bright red; the eyes with long false lashes, too much mascara underneath and on top as well as on her eyebrows. Everything is overdone. The sight is absurd and in another sense pathetic. I smother a giggle.

"You can laugh," she cries. "And look at this." And she holds a foot up displaying a high heeled mauve shoe, shiny, bright, gaudy. She loses her balance and grabs hold of the cupboard door for support. The shoe falls off. "And this," she screeches deforming her face with thumb and fingers. "What do I look like? If my father could see me he would turn in his grave. You've made me into a dishcloth, a cipher, a fat round zero, that's what you've done."

"I didn't ask you to dress up as a clown."

"But it amused you didn't it?"

I grin: "I can't deny you did give me a laugh."

"You're a brute. That part of your nature your sister got right."

"I'm sorry Rita. I confess I haven't treated you too well."

"Too well?" she cries. "You've treated me abominably. A dog wouldn't have put up with some of the things I've stuck from you."

"Forgive me." I try and take her by the shoulders, but she shrugs me away.

"I must be going," she says.

"When do I see you again?"

"Everything between us is finished."

"I think you mean it, Rita," I said turning her face towards me, looking her straight in the eyes. "Something has happened I know. What is it? I want to get to the bottom of it. Why have you suddenly changed?"

She bows her head a little, avoids my stare, "Au revoir, Peter." And she struggles to put her coat on. I help her and escort her to the door. A few minutes later, from the window, five stories high, I watch the tiny figure moving down the road. There are tears in my eyes. I sense this rupture is not like the others. Then I reassure myself: she'll be back; it is not the first time we have broken off.

The windows are wide open. It is bright and sunny outside. London's delicious polluted air is floating in the room. Yet it smells, not of oil, car exhausts, industrial fumes, but plain household filth — stale food, soiled linen, un-emptied trash cans, dirt and dust. The air freshener I have bought has sort of superimposed its own odorless odor into the atmosphere giving me the feeling that I am inhaling purified, disinfected, non-toxic air. The bed is unmade; clothes, newspapers, towels, shoes, and much else invisible to the naked eye, are strewn about the floor; a pile of dirty washing is stacked by the little electric heater; my desk is in a disgusting mess — papers, books, pills, pins, peanuts, glue, jam and God knows what. This is the clutter and filth I have been living in for over a week. I am, putting it crudely, living in my own shit. Now and again I have attempted to do a mini spring-clean, but it is always half-hearted and I do a lousy job. On several occasions I have been tempted to ring Rita, but I have refrained. I felt sure she would show signs of life before now. But nothing. Meanwhile the stink is getting unbearable. I stifle my pride and dial her number. There are limits to even what I can endure.

"Rita, how are you?" I greet her cheerfully. "What's become of you?"

"What do you want Peter?" she whispers.

"I want to see you."

"It's impossible."

"What's happened Rita?" I ask anxiously. "Are you ill?"

"I'm very well thank you Peter. It is very nice of you to enquire after my health."

"Why are you speaking like a pompous ass?"

"Good-bye Peter." And I hear the click in the receiver.

I dial again and this time she tells me in a hoarse angry whisper not call again. The line goes dead.

I quickly slip my coat on and a few minutes later I am briskly walking down the street towards her flat. A thousand disjointed thoughts skip pell-mell through my mind. I am annoyed and frustrated. I don't understand what has happened. Is Rita trying to be tough? Has she stopped loving me? Why, the sudden change in her? I can't believe our relationship has fizzled out, died like the slam of a door. There must he a reason, a perfectly simple explanation. I must get to the bottom of it all.

Down the street there is a curious melee of people, all ages, nationalities, colors. Central London has become a melting pot of the Commonwealth. I like the area because it is so cosmopolitan, bustling and alive. There are always people about — shopping, strolling, standing around. Several street vendors are selling knickknacks out of suit cases — stockings, scarves, silverware, gimmicks of one sort or another. For a couple of minutes I stop and watch a guy doing card tricks (with bets) on an upturned fruit box. The block of flats is huge and modern, though the entrance is small. The porter, all in black — cap, suit, tie — knows me well and says something about the weather as he presses the button for the lift. A moment later I am impatiently ringing Rita's bell. She opens the door, but when she sees me her eyes flash nervously and her face sort of goes rigid. "I told you not to come," she hisses.

"I want to see you." I smile uncertainly.

"Go away."

I put my foot in the door. Rita is wearing a dark blue dress. Maybe a new one, for it has a neat glow about it, inconceivable of her older stuff even if it had just come from the cleaners. Her hair is done up in a bun (as she always had it), though trim as though she had recently been to the hairdresser. Gone is the powder, paint and perfume. She wears no makeup at all. The flat smells clean with disinfectant.

"Who is it?" a voice calls from the sitting room.

"Peter," she replies, her voice slightly high pitched.

"Peter. Peter. Come in."

Rita makes way for me, (To some extent I brush her aside.) I go into the sitting room and there I get the shock of my life. I don't believe in ghosts and yet I am seeing one: tall and thickset, the face, though a little older, is unmistakable. I feel I am going to pass out: my legs are shaking; there is an unpleasant contraction in my stomach; I feel nauseous. Thick podgy hands give me a firm handshake.

"Well, well, good to see you Peter. But you look as if you've seen a ghost. Sit down."

I flop into an easy chair.

"Cyril returned from Australia a few days ago," explains Rita rapidly. "He was thinking we might live there and was testing the territory. But now he thinks it would be better if we remained in England, which we know, with all the conveniences — theaters, concerts, comforts that money can buy."

Cyril cuts her short imperiously, as though he was telling her to shut up: "Australia is not for us. It is for young people. It is a country with many possibilities, vast natural resources, plenty of room for expansion and development. But we belong to the old world with its slower pace of life, its traditions, its more sophisticated people, etc etc. Rita what are you waiting for? Get some tea and biscuits. Make Peter feel welcome." She scurries out of the room. He goes on talking.

Cyril only looks a little older. His face is redder, more lined, with heavier rings around the eyes. The hair, what there is of it, is brilliantined to his scalp. If I recall correctly it is thinner, greyer, but now he has side whiskers which he didn't have before. He is dressed eccentrically as of old: brown trousers, dark green waist coat, yellow shirt, green and yellow striped tie. A purple jacket is over the back of a chair. In a loud rasping voice he is telling me about Australia, the Australians, what he did, what he saw. I am only half listening. I am dying to get to Rita, to get her on her own, to hear what she has to say.

"I'll go and see if I can help Rita," I rapidly inject at the first lull in the monologue, struggling to my feet.

"Leave her be," he waves me to sit down again. "Don't get her into bad habits. If you help her she might expect me to. As it is I never set foot in the kitchen. That's the woman's domain. Take my advice, if ever you get married never give a helping hand as you call it. Once you start, it never ends. The man has his work; the woman hers. Don't let her confuse you about this."

A little later, when we are all sipping tea, gently munching biscuits, politely talking about this and that, very much like in the old days, Cyril excuses himself, presumably to go to the toilet. "Why didn't you tell me he wasn't dead?" I whisper reproachfully as soon as he is out of earshot.

No answer. She looks down at the carpet, avoiding my stare. Her face is white, puffy, wrinkled. It is like a badly made mask made of *papier maché*. The expression is sort of blank and betrays no emotion, or movement. This is the Rita I remember before going to Mégève, anyway when her husband was around. I want to tell her it is not me that has made her into a doormat: she always was one. Other words, however, more pressing, come bubbling out.

"He ran away from you didn't he? You were too proud to admit it. But then, somehow or other, he heard about the inheritance. That's why you were so nervous isn't it? I'm right aren't I?"

She looks at me, through me would be more accurate and says coldly: "You don't understand anything."

Cyril returns, shaking his hands and wrists, flicking his fingers. "You forgot to put towels out in the bathroom, Rita."

"I'll get them." She hurries out.

GEORGE

Part I

"I'd rather die than give you David."

He hit her, a resounding slap. She staggered backwards nursing her cheek, her long white face frigid with fear or fury. She contained her emotion.

"You stupid woman. You don't know what you're saying. Where would David be without me?… You too for that matter. I didn't have to marry you. I did it out of sympathy to give you respectability, because you were getting old. You were on the shelf. You were, weren't you?

"Must you with David in the room?" she whispered hoarsely. He yelled at the boy to get the hell out of the place and go to his room.

"Well," he reiterated; "I hope I've made myself clear. You can go, in fact I'll be glad to see the back of you. You can have a divorce just as soon as the lawyers are ready; but David stays. I've got his future to think of and you're not fit to have him." He made a move towards the bathroom, but stopped and turned. "And just in case you have any ideas I've got a court order out forbidding you to take him out of the Bahamas. So if you want a divorce you sign him over to me. Otherwise the status quo. I don't particularly like seeing you, but if I must I can put up with the present arrangement."

He slammed the bathroom door. Emily went and slumped in a chair. She had a long thin body. She wore no make-up and her skin was pale, crinkly and close up betrayed her 35 years. Her features, however, were attractive: fair with blue eyes, straight nose, thin lips, high cheek bones her beauty was classical. At a party, suitably decked up for the occasion, in dim light, she was stunning.

George came out of the bathroom. "I forgot to tell you that I don't want you to go to meditation any more. It's your job to baby sit, not mine. I don't mind doing it now and again, but you've been abusing. Do you know that in the last week you've had three late nights? That's neither right nor fair."

He stood in the middle of the room feet akimbo, hands on hips. He had a bullet of a head, mostly bald, forehead tanned by the sun, the rest of his face was red, as though he was a drinker. As usual he wore T-shirt and shorts. He looked at her threateningly, as though he wanted her to reply, so he could have the opportunity to slam her down. But she kept silent, only staring at him with cold hatred.

"I have nothing against you going to yoga," he went on: "In fact I think the exercise very good for you. It's the meditation. I've heard a lot of nasty things about it."

"What have you heard?" she asked crisply, stirring from her apathy.

"That they're just pot sessions."

"That's not true," she protested angrily.

"You're not going to tell me you meditate until one o'clock in the morning?"

"No. After meditation we chant a little, somebody gives a talk, then we sit and chat."

"Well, whatever you do I don't want you to go any more. In a small place like Nassau people talk and I don't want my name mixed up with that kind of thing. I've got my reputation to think of."

"Tonight Joe is giving a party and I promised I'd go."

"You can ring up and say you're very sorry, you can't make it."

"I won't do it."

He stuck his chest out, a mass of hairs visible under the shirt. "Don't you understand, Emily? You're a married woman, with duties and responsibilities. Towards your son. Towards me... All right, even if I mean nothing to you there's David. You can't expect me to look after him all the time.'

"It's what you're asking for if I turned him over to you, isn't it?"

His nostrils flared. "That's not the same at all. If he were entirely my responsibility I'd make different arrangements. I'd have a woman full time to look after him. But with you in the house it's not possible."

"I don't see why not. I've always wanted a maid."

"'You stupid woman, I'm not talking about a maid. I'm talking about a mistress. Though I'm 59 I'm vigorous and strong. There's many a woman who would be glad to fit into the little niche I could offer her. But I want you to know that as long as you're my wife I'll remain faithful and provide for you. I realize my obligations even if you don't."

Emily got up and left the house. George trailed after her, abusing her — telling her she was impossible, selfish, immature. She ignored him and getting into her car drove away.

She went straight round to Joe He had come into her life three months earlier when she had started yoga. Mild, sensitive intellectual — he was the antithesis of George. To Emily be had been a revelation. For the first time in her life she discovered she could be herself.

When he opened the door she fell into his arms. For a few moments they held each other tight. She had tears in her eyes. She could feel her pent up anger dissolving. She loved Joe. Though they had never discussed it she felt, and tacitly assumed, he would marry her if she was free. If it had not been for David she would have run away with him.

Joe was 37, tall, lanky with a long sallow face, his head was balding on top. He had light brown eyes, full lips. He was the associate editor of the Nassau Telegraph.

She disengaged herself. "Joe I'm going mad. I don't know what I'll do if I have to live with that monster any longer."

"Tell me about it," he said gently.

She told him.

"I'm sure the courts will give you custody of David."

"I'm not at all sure. This is the Bahamas. Things don't work here like any normal country. Then George has a strong case. He's got the money; he can provide for him much better than I can; can give him more opportunities, a better education. Then, as he rightly, points out, we were only able to adopt him because we were a partnership. And as George never stops reminding me he was the kingpin in the partnership because of his wealth and standing in the community."

"Yes, but didn't you tell me that after Doctor Bethel had seen you and put you both through that battery of psychological tests, he recommended that you should get David?"

She shrugged. "The report says I'm immature, repressed, not very responsible. That won't sound very impressive to a judge.'"

"I think you're looking on the black side. The report also says that George is aggressive with paranoiac tendencies and possibilities of latent homosexuality. No judge in his right mind would ignore that. Besides, whatever you like to say, Bethel still recommended that you get custody of the boy."

She gave him a hug and beamed. "You always manage to say just the right thing. I don't know what I would do if I couldn't come here and let off steam."

"Lie on your stomach Emily and I'll give you a little massage. You're still very tense."

She did what he said and with delicate long fingers he set to work on her, and soon she felt so relaxed that she began to feel drowsy. Then, like a lazy cat, she rolled over on her back. She lifted her lips for him to kiss. He pecked at them and smiled. He then helped her to her feet, took her in his arms and again kissed and hugged her.

"I think you should go to yoga," he said drawing away. "It's nearly time." He then added that he wouldn't come as he had to prepare for the party.

"I'll stay and help you," she replied.

Two hours later he reminded her it was time for her to go home."

"See you later." she said at the door.

"Do you think it wise after what he said?"

She smiled thinly and nodded. "Don't worry. I'll be here."

When she got home George was standing in the middle of the room waiting for her. His bullet head glistened in the light. She felt he was going to charge. Her knees began to wobble."

"I know all about Joe," he came straight to the point. "I didn't want to say so earlier, but I've had my suspicions for a long time. You don't really think I believed all that rot about meditation do you? Do you think I don't know where you go running off to at every opportunity? And where you've just come from. And don't tell me you've been to yoga. I know damn well you haven't. No matter. All I want to know is have you been unfaithful to me?"

She looked at him frigidly, then replied softly: "No."

"Very well. Let us keep temptation at bay. I forbid you to do any more yoga and you must stop seeing this Joe creep completely. I don't want people talking. I hope I make myself clear."

She went into the kitchen and quickly prepared a hamburger dinner.

George told her he would be going to a sailing club meeting and would not be back until late. She called David and told him to wash his hands, ready for dinner.

A few moments later he appeared and scrambled on a chair. He was a fair little boy with bright rosy cheeks and blue eyes. Until recently he had been perky and mischievous. The last few months, however, as things visibly deteriorated between his parents, he had become more subdued. Now he sat silent waiting for his food.

Immediately after the meal George went out. Emily rang for a babysitter. Then she went and said goodnight to David. She told him a little story, hugged and kissed him. "You're mummy's baby." And she felt a glow of warmth swell up within her. "How would you like a new daddy?"'she added lightly.

He stared at her with his wide blue eyes.

"A daddy who would tell you stories, play games with you, take you and mummy for drives…"

"Will he hit you mummy?"

She laughed softly: "No."

She then kissed him again and left him.

Half an hour later she was at Joe's. The door was open and she went in. Already there were quite a few people. Mostly the yoga crowd. In the background you could hear Indian music. A smell of incense pervaded the air. The goodies on the table were vegetarian — salads, fruits, nuts, various cheeses and breads. Somebody came up to her and offered her a celery and carrot juice.

"I didn't think you'd be coming," said Joe suddenly appearing.

She smiled: "I told you I'd make it didn't I?"

Your husband rang up and said he didn't want us to see each other anymore. I think for everybody's sake it would be better if you weren't seen here."

"You're not serious Joe?"

He nodded: "I don't think you should do anything in haste now which you might regret later."

Emily was a little confused. She didn't know what to say, so she said nothing. Joe went to attend to some other guests. She lingered a few moments, then decided she had better go. Perhaps Joe was right? Somebody was bound to tell George she had been at the party. Nevertheless, Joe had made her feel insecure. She resolved to have it out with him later.

For a while she drove aimlessly. Then she stopped for a drink. Normally she drank little, but that night she downed four whiskies. She returned to Joe's, but the party was still going strong so she crept away. She'd have to see Joe another time. When she got home it was nearly midnight. She paid the babysitter and went to bed.

It must have been less than five minutes later when George pounced in her room and switched on her light: "Where have been?" he demanded.

"What is it, George?" she said sitting up in bed, rubbing her eyes.

"Don't pretend I've just woken you up. I know you've been somewhere. The engine of your car is still warm."

"I've been out," she answered coldly.

"Have you been round to that little creep?"

She didn't answer.

"Did he tell you what he told me? That he wouldn't marry you, had no intention of marrying you, even if you were free."

She paled. She began to shiver. "I... I... I don't believe you," she faltered. "You're just telling me that because... because you don't want me to see him any more, to hurt me... because you want to be nasty."

George laughed. "Ring the creep up and see for yourself."

"I'm going round to see him," she said getting out of bed.

Twenty minutes later she was banging at his door. The guests had gone, but he was still up. She fell into his arms. "Tell me it's not true." she begged. "He just wanted to hurt me."

She had to explain what she was talking about. When she had finished he took her in his arms. "Emily, I was thinking of you and David. I can't keep you in the style of life you are accustomed to. I'd hate myself if I made you miserable."

"Joe, tell me you love me."

"Of course I love you." And he kissed her.

She gave a deep sigh and abandoned herself to his embrace. Eventually feeling a little suffocated he pulled away. "I think you'd better be going now Emily," he said.

"Joe, I want you to make love to me," and she turned towards the bedroom. He hesitated and she sensed his hesitation. "Come. Show me you love me." She took his hand.

"This is all wrong."

She tugged his arm.

Very shortly afterwards she left Joe. The whole business had embarrassed him. He didn't want to get involved. He liked Emily well enough. In fact he was very fond of her, but physically she didn't attract him. He liked to chat with her, exchange confidences and in her (a married woman) he thought he had the ideal woman for a Platonic relationship. He had told her he loved her because he had seen how distraught she was. Right or wrong he didn't want to hurt her. Anyhow, the evening, he determined, was a memory best forgotten. He went to bed.

Several hours later, though to Joe it seemed like minutes, he was abruptly awakened by the phone ringing. It was George: "Emily says it's happened," the voice spat. "Is it true?"

Joe was perplexed. Emily had left hours ago. He denied everything."I think you're a liar," George shouted. "I've been waiting up for her and she's just this minute come in. What's more she's confessed everything."

"Nothing's true," repeated Joe.

"Don't give me that shit."

"You might at least be civil."

"Civil… When you've just made a cuckold of me. You've got to be joking."

"Can I see you?"

"Whatever for?…If I saw you I'd probably punch your head."

"Why did you ring me?"

"I… I… I just wanted to tell you you can have my wife. Good riddance to her. I've kicked her out. She's coming to you at once." He slammed down the receiver.

Light was breaking when she got round to Joe, for perhaps the tenth time in the last twenty four hours. She knocked on his door. No answer. She banged a little louder, called his name. Where could he be, she wondered? At that time of morning there were few places to go. Then it struck her perhaps he didn't want to see her. The thought frightened her. She had to talk to him. She could explain everything. Primarily she wanted to tell him she would accept anything. But he had to take her and David away.

Soon she realized he wasn't going to let her in and she drove to the nearest hotel. She phoned him. No reply. She sat in the lobby for half an hour; then rang again. Same result. She was feeling wretched. She shouldn't have pushed him, she thought, But she was desperate. Didn't he realize how desperate she was? She telephoned several more times. Finally, she conceded defeat and with a heavy heart returned home.

The door was bolted from the inside. She rang. George came to the window and told her if she had come for her things to collect them when he was out. "I don't want to see you any more."

"We're still married," she replied.

There was a pause. He grunted. Then went to the front door and let her in. "I suppose as long as you're still my wife I'll have to let you live in the house … But understand, while you're here you'll have to perform your marital duties. I hope I make myself clear."

She nodded meekly. She felt sick and exhausted. She flopped into a chair.

"Well, did you see Joe?"

She nodded.

"And what did he say?"

"He's going to marry me," she mumbled.

George went up to her and gave her a hard slap on the face. "You filthy little liar. And to think I've put up with you all this time."' She stared at him in shock. "You want me to believe you've just seen Joe, when I know damn well you haven't. You're simply a pack of lies. I don't believe a word you say. And you have the nerve to claim you're fit to look after David. You're mad, Emily. And so is that crackpot analyst who thinks you should get custody of him."

"How … How did you know I hadn't seen Joe?" she stammered.

"Because he's here, that's why. Arrived almost as soon as you left. I'm a fair man. I decided I'd hear his end of the story, so I rang and told him to come round. He was hopping mad with you, I can tell you that. I could see he wasn't play acting… Why in heaven's name, woman, did you have to tell me you had been unfaithful. What were you trying to accomplish? Did you want to give me a heart attack or something?"

"I was thinking of David," she muttered. "I thought if you knew I had been unfaithful you would let me go and Joe would take me once I had your blessing."

George scratched his head. "You're off your rocker, woman. You can't even think straight. What did you expect? Did you think I'd say 'yes dear, you can have a divorce: it's all my fault and you can take David'… And did you think Joe would take you both just like that? Didn't he tell you he wouldn't marry you? That's what he's just told me anyway."

Emily was speechless. Inside she felt numb, as though she was all dried up. Her life was falling apart and she knew it. She was half-inclined to believe George— that she was mad. And if not, fast going that way. She wanted to say Joe loved her. He didn't want to marry her because he couldn't provide for her, not in the way she was used to.

"Haven't you a tongue in your head, woman? Have you nothing to say?"

She stared vacantly in front of her. George called Joe, who came out of the next room. "Tell her why you won't marry her," he said.

He hesitated and then barely audible replied: "Emily, I'm already committed."

Her eyes flickered, but she registered no expression.

"Leave her," said George. "Come. I should be grateful if you would massage my back again. You're really very good. Then we can go and have breakfast at the Country Club. And if you're feeling up to it we can play a round of golf."

* * * * *

Part II

George and Joe had arranged to meet for lunch at the Country Club. Over the last few weeks they had often lunched together, but always in town. It was 12:30 when Joe parked his car and made his way to the restaurant. George was already waiting for him.

"I thought it would be quieter here," George greeted him with a wide smile, as though delighted to see him.

Joe slipped into a seat.

"I think Emily is just about to crack," the older man began immediately. "This analyst I was telling you about has agreed to come over from Miami tomorrow. He's going to stay with us next weekend. See us both together, how we live, the real thing. I spoke to Emily's attorney this morning. He thinks it's a good idea. But I have a shrewd suspicion he thinks the whole thing will backfire. That he'll also recommend Emily get custody of David. But I don't think that'll happen."

About a week earlier the three of them had thrashed the whole thing out at the house. George had asked Joe along for support. The old man had been a model of reasonableness: he said he was only thinking of the boy; he honestly believed that Emily wasn't fit to look after him; he saw no harm in getting a second expert opinion. Then they knew the doctor and Emily had previously consulted with him.

Joe, though just as eager as George to see the back of Emily wanted to appear impartial. That was the best approach, he thought. So he listened. Emily said she didn't like the doctor, thought him a crook and would say anything George told him to. Joe gently protested. He repeated George's arguments and some more of his own. But she had been adamant and in the end Joe had bluntly told her she was unreasonable. Joe had agreed to move into the house with George just as soon as she was gone. A live-in maid would look after David.

Drinks were served and they ordered the special.

"I don't see why she should cooperate," said Joe as soon as the waitress was out of earshot.

George shrugged: "She doesn't have to agree; but I don't think it matters. The point is both Bethel and her attorney are on my side. She's got nobody to turn to. That's why I think she's cracking. Before, she could always run to you. Now she's got to bottle it all up inside. And God knows she's pretty repressed anyway… To be quite honest I really do believe she's hinged."

"Supposing this analyst thinks she should get custody of the boy?"

George eyes twinkled. "He won't."

"I don't see how you can be so sure."

Food was brought and they helped themselves in silence.

"It's a good thing I rang her attorney," said George with a mouthful."The little bitch told me that her attorney didn't approve of the idea. I really can't make her out. Does she think I'm stupid or something? All I had to do was pick up the receiver and talk to the man.

"I saw her yesterday at the supermarket and she really did look over-wrought. She actually looked sick."

"It's her own damn fault. She's asked for it. Anyway, in a few days I reckon it will all be over. She'll either go or have a nervous breakdown. And all her stupid stubbornness will have amounted to nothing."

Joe kept quiet, but he didn't entirely share George's cocksureness.

A couple of hours later, he was back at the paper. George called him. There was a note of urgency in his voice: "Listen Joe, she's gone. And the bloody bitch has taken David with her."

Joe gave a soft whistle. Then asked what made him so certain.

"There's a note, but I don't like to talk on the phone Can you come round as soon as you finish work?"

"I'll be as quick as I can."

Shortly after six o'clock George opened the door and let Joe in.

"I must admit I didn't think the silly bitch would have the guts,"George said, letting Joe follow him into the sitting room. "It's what she should have done ages ago if she'd got any sense. But she's not going to get away with it. That I assure you."

"Can I see the note?"

George took it off a shelf next to some books and handed it to him. "It doesn't say very much, but enough."

The note said: "I'VE TAKEN DAVID". That was all. No signature.

"What do you propose to do?" asked Joe.

"I've checked all the hotels and she's not putting up at any of them. I've been on to the airlines and they are going through their passenger lists. I should be hearing from them any minute. Pan Am and Eastern already called back and said she wasn't on any of their flights."

"She might be staying with friends."

"That's a possibility, but I doubt it. There's nobody she knows here whom I don't know. She's got friends in Freeport, but not here, none that would play her game anyway."

"Have you rung these people you say she knows in Freeport?"

"No. I don't know who they are."

At that moment the phone rang. George grabbed it, listened for a minute or two and replaced the receiver. "Delta ... Nothing. That leaves only the local airlines. Trust them to be the slowest."

"Has Emily got any money?"

"Not much. I know she's got a few thousand pounds in England. That's about it, except of course what she's got on her which can't be much."

For a few moments the two men were silent. Joe sat in the rocking chair. George paced up and down the room, the bullet part of his head thrust forward shining, as though it had been polished.

"You've just given me an idea," he said stopping, turning towards Joe. "I'm going to get her money frozen in England. If she's broken a court order here the British authorities should help, anyway to start with." He went over to the phone and dialed a number. When he got through his attorney wasn't in, so he left a message to ring back urgently.

"And if Emily comes back what will you do?"

"Nothing at all. Treat the whole thing as though it had

never happened. Go through the normal procedures we were already going through before she took it into her silly head to run away."

"'And if she leaves or has left the country what then?"

"That's why I want to freeze her assets. Without money she won't be able to get very far. She can perhaps put up with relations for a short time, but come what may she's going to need hard cash. And I'll damn well see that she doesn't get a release on her account until we've been through the courts or I get David back."

The phone rang. George answered, and smiling put down the receiver."She took Outer Island Airways to Freeport.'"

"Does that mean you're going to follow her?"

"No. That's what she'd expect. She'll probably lie low for a few days. Looking for her would be like searching for a pin in the grass. But I've got a little idea. It's a shot in the dark, but if I know Emily she won't go rushing off to England immediately. She's already taken one big step leaving here, taking David. I suspect she'll want a breather, to think things over, discuss the matter with her friends before embarking on any further action... Anyway, I have a little plan."

He looked very pleased with himself and going over to the table picked up the afternoon paper. "It's going to be a nice day tomorrow," he said.

"What are you going to do?" asked Joe.

"I'm going sailing. That's what I'm going to do."

"Sailing? ... what's that got to do with Emily and David?"

Striding across the room George clapped and rubbed his hands. "Everything is going to be just fine," he cried. Then added lightly: "If I didn't know you hated sailing I'd ask you to join me."

Again the phone rang. Joe sat perplexed as George spoke to his attorney. It was a long conversation. Joe could see the attorney wasn't telling him what he wanted to hear. Eventually, scowling, he hung up.

"Blasted red tape. The lawyer says I can't do anything about freezing her account in England as long as she's in The Bahamas and hasn't broken the court injunction." Then he added more breezily: "Still, if my scheme comes off none of that will matter."

Then, and later over dinner, Joe pressed him for more information. But each time George laughed and told him he had better not tell him because he might not approve. Afterwards, he said, they would both have a good laugh.

The next day was a Saturday and Joe's day off. No paper came out on the Sunday, which meant that the editorial staff didn't work Saturdays. That evening he had gone to the pictures on his own. He had called George several times to get him to come along, but there had been no reply. On the Sunday he drifted into the newsroom around eleven o'clock.

A few minutes later he had been jolted out of his customary Sunday morning lethargy. The news was that George Farfield was missing. He had gone sailing the previous morning and had not returned. Search parties had been working from late evening and throughout the night. They were still working, and would continue throughout the day.

Shortly after lunch there was a surge of excitement. George's dingy had been found. Joe, who was in constant touch with BASRA (Bahamas Air Sea Rescue Association) made notes. And it was while he was scribbling that a thought struck him. George had said it was going to be a nice day. Yet it had been wet, windy and the sea had looked pretty rough.

By nightfall a spokesman from BASRA said the search had been abandoned. The area where the boat was found had been scoured. No hope was offered. The spokesman said that, though George was a good sailor, there was little chance of his surviving once the dingy had capsized. Nevertheless they had continued to search for a period well beyond the dictates of reason.

Joe began the story for the paper, but found he was too upset to complete it. He told a reporter to do it. It was suddenly beginning to dawn on Joe that he would never see George again. He felt sad and empty, very tired. It struck him as a curious twist of fate that Emily would get David after all. George probably hadn't even had time to disinherit them. Nor, he reflected, would he ever know his friend's master plan. All very ironic. And perfect for Emily. It was as though she had cast a spell.

That night he took a couple of sleeping pills before going to bed.

Emily caught the last flight back to Nassau on the Tuesday evening. She had seen the news in the Monday's paper and again heard it over the radio. It hadn't required much thought for her to make up her mind. Legally she was still George's wife. And heir. The most natural thing for her to do would be to act normally, as though she had only gone away for an extended weekend.

She had a strange feeling letting herself into the house — silent, slightly musty, exactly how George had left it. She skipped across the sitting room, gave a little cry of joy. David watched her curious and perplexed. "Where's daddy?" he asked. She told him he had gone away and wouldn't be back for a long long time.

Emily wore black. No powder, perfume, lipstick. The night before she had taken numerous black coffees. She didn't want to sleep. She wanted to look tired and haggard, a woman broken down by sorrow. But the role she had prepared for herself didn't quite come off. Underneath you sensed an electrifying aliveness, notwithstanding the pale face, blood-shot eyes, the slightly puffy cheeks.

She prepared herself and David a snack, bathed him, put

him to bed. A funeral service was to be held the following morning at eleven o'clock and she wanted him to look fresh and rosy, a credit to herself if not George. She sung him a little song, told him a story, made him say his prayers. Then for a short while she lovingly watched over him as he melted away into dreamland.

She had a bath, prepared herself coffee, tried to get something on television. But reception was bad so she switched it off and went to bed. She read a little and around 2:00 a.m. turned the lights off.

A few minutes later, or it seemed that way to her, she stirred abruptly. A pang of fear ran through her. There was a noise outside the room. She hadn't been dreaming, she was sure. She listened expectantly clutching the sheet, staring into the darkness. A thief she thought: he thinks the house is empty. A cupboard opened and closed. Let him take what he wants, she told herself. But then David began crying and, without thinking, she leapt out of bed.

She opened her door and just as she did so the lights in the hallway went on. She screamed. The brightness dazzled her and at first she saw nothing. Then a moment later she saw quite clearly — the stocky figure, the bullet head, the face flushed and grinning.

"I've come for some clothes. I'm going to a funeral later today. I've got to be well dressed."

She gaped, paralyzed with horror.

"I've also come for David."

"This is a trick," she gasped. "A trick to get me here... and... and... you."

"You must admit Emily, a brilliant idea."

"'Where's David?" she cried, a note of terror in her voice. But her adrenalin was beginning to flow. She made a move towards the boy's room. George blocked her way.

"No, Emily."

"You're not going to get him," she yelled.

"Who's going to stop me?"

Emily dashed into the kitchen and emerged holding a carving knife. "Go away George," she screeched.

He laughed: "Put that thing down, Emily. Don't be ridiculous."

He tried to grab the instrument, but she wouldn't let him get near her and she struck out. George, his hands and fingers dripping with blood, became livid. He flung his arms at her and managed to seize a wrist, which he promptly started twisting. She screamed and with her free hand lashed out hysterically. She felt the knife sink into something soft. There was a groan. His grip slackened.

Like a tiger, she hurled herself at him. She plunged the knife into him, once, twice; and when he fell on the floor she fell on top of him. She struck him again and again. And even when he was no longer resisting she continued to hit him. She was weeping and screaming, ejaculating strange animalistic cries. Then suddenly she stopped, looked at the blade, her bloody hands, the bleeding gashes all over George's body.

For a few moments she stood mesmerized by the ghastly scene. Then slowly she became aware of the screaming, not George, not herself, but David. He was standing in the passage, watching, clinging to the door handle of his room, his little face red, wet, convulsed with wailing. Emily dropped the knife, rushed to him. "Come dear… It's nothing… nothing at all. Just a bad dream. Nobody is going to hurt you … Everything is going to be all right."

She took him in her arms and gently began to rock him. He put his thumb in his mouth, curled himself up, buried his head in her bosom. But it was quite a time before he began to calm down. And much longer still before he fell asleep and she was able to put him back to bed.

Some hours later (when it was already dawn) she wrapped the body in several blankets and put it in a trunk. She cleared up the mess. She would have to think how to dispose of the body later. Now she wanted a little rest before getting ready for Church.

Emily and David wore black. There were quite a lot of people at the service. George had been a popular figure in Nassau. Joe had very briefly spoken to Emily before the majority of people had begun to arrive. She was ashen pale. She looked sick. He had never seen her so distraught. She could barely speak. David too was shaken.

Joe couldn't make Emily out. If she was play-acting she was putting on a damn good show. He couldn't believe it. Something was odd. And why had she pulled David away so quickly when he had started talking about a nightmare? She's definitely disturbed, he thought. George was right.

Then he started thinking about his friend. He couldn't get out of his mind what he had said about the weather — 'a nice day'. But it had been wet and windy, exactly as forecast. That wasn't like George at all. Something was wrong, very wrong. He didn't know what to do. He had lost a friend, more than a friend. He stared with bitterness through his tears at the woman who, he felt, was somehow responsible for it all.

THE CHARMER

THE BED-SITTER IS IN A grey, late Victorian, building five minutes walk from University College. It is early spring and though crisp and sunny Charles has the light on. When he is home (and not asleep) he always has the light on, for the room overlooks the interior of the building and is forever dark. Somewhere below there is some corrugated iron and when it rains the noise is infernal, like hail thrashing the hood of a car.

The room itself, medium sized, is like thousands of others in the area: the wallpaper shearing; the rugs and drapes tattered and tawny; the furniture cheap, utilitarian and down the corridor a primitive but functional bathroom.

But this particular room is more chilling than most. It is untidy, dirty and dusty. There are no pictures, no photographs, no ornaments—none of those knickknacks which most people collect on their journey through life. Nor is a radio, tape-deck, record player or television apparent. The only distinguishing thing about the room are the books, hundreds of them (maybe thousands) — large heavy tomes stacked haphazardly everywhere and anywhere. Many are dark with age, dusty, as though they hadn't been handled for an eternity. The impression you got is that of a used seedy book store, not somebody's home.

The books are mainly on International Affairs, Economics, History, Politics, Philosophy. Here and there, there is a smattering of biography — biographies mostly of military men, politicians, reformers, religious leaders. What fiction there is (and there's very little) is in paperback and gives the impression it got into the room by accident. There is no poetry, no humor, nothing on art.

Charles has been living in the room just over nine months. He is a student, 20, studying history. He is tall, strongly built, very fair; his hair has a tendency to flop over his right eye and he is constantly flicking his head back (or running a hand over his forehead) to clear his vision. His jaw is firm; the mouth shuts tightly; the eyes are blue-grey and hard. The teeth are straight and very white, but when he smiles you get the impression of a grimace, a plastic smirk, as though he isn't laughing with you but at you.

Charles is sitting at his desk, looking through a pile of papers. A pencil is in his hand and he chews the end from time to time. Occasionally he jots something down. Less frequently he looks at his watch. He is wearing slacks, open necked shirt, sneakers. The room is cool, but he doesn't appear to notice the temperature. There is a knock on the door. He looks up, but doesn't answer. Deliberately he continues reading, note taking. The knock is repeated: once, twice, three times. "Are you there, Charles?"

"Is that you Alec?"

"Yes."

"Hang on. I won't be a moment."

Charles quickly gets up and seems to do everything at once. He throws the cover over the unmade bed, smooths it down, picks up some papers, clothes, slippers and other oddments from the floor, tosses them into a cupboard, shuts it and locks it. He throws a quick glance round the room, then satisfied it isn't in too much of a mess, opens the door.

Alec is wearing a dark blue coat, buttoned up, the creases in the right places, all very smart looking as though it was new or had just come from the cleaners. A wide toothy smile is already on his face when the door opens. His eyes are sparkling a friendly clear blue. "Glad to see you Charles. It's been ages." He puts out his hand.

Charles ignores it and doesn't even smile. "Come in. Find yourself a seat. Sorry about the mess. I've been working."

Alec removes his coat. He is wearing a grey suit, waistcoat, white shirt (stiff collar), old school tie. Like Charles he is fair, but looks a little younger. Around his mouth are faint creases — lines of self discipline or from smiling too much. The lower part of his face appears delicate: the chin small, slightly receding; the lips sensitive and sensually red. The cheeks are high, but somewhat bony giving him a withdrawn look, perhaps even effeminate. A beard and moustache on the face would make him look much tougher, more of a 'he-man'.

Alec, still holding his coat, doesn't sit down, but looks at Charles. He continues to smile. "You're looking fine," he says. "I've never seen you looking so well."

Charles grunts and flicking his hair out of his eyes goes and sits behind his desk. Alec sits on the bed. He adjusts himself finding an even part on the cover. Charles stares at him like a prospective interviewee. Alec shifts nervously. He has always been a little uneasy with Charles, he doesn't quite know why. He puts his coat next to the pillow and forces himself to say something: "Well Charles, tell me about yourself."

"Nothing to say. As you see I'm up to my neck in work."

"How's it going?"

"Fine. I do twelve hours a day."

"That's a hell of a lot."

Charles scowls. "Merely a question of will training. The harder I work the easier it becomes."

"I admire your tenacity." Then after a pause: "How long have you been here? I mean in this room."

"Since August."

"Why didn't you tell us where you were living?"

"I didn't want to be disturbed."

A frown appears on Alec's forehead. "From your work you mean?"

"From my work."

Pause.

"I must say Charles we were a little bit surprised by your sudden change. I still don't understand why you chose to cut us dead."

"I told you I had work to do."

"That's hardly a reason for dropping your friends." He hesitates. Charles registers no emotion. Alec's face widens into a broad grin. "Still that's over and done with now. I'm glad you got in touch with me."

"If you think I got in touch with you because I want to renew old acquaintances you're mistaken."

Alec frowns. The smile vanishes. He is silent. He waits expectantly for Charles to go on, to provide some sort of explanation. But Charles says nothing. He scrutinizes Alec as though he was a freak. Alec drops his eyes down and again shifts nervously. Why does he always feel like an insect when he's with Charles?

"Why did you ask me round here if you don't want to see any of us again?" he asks at length.

"I didn't say I didn't want to see you again." He emphasized the "you". "I was talking about the others."

"We were all friends together."

"WERE."

Alec laughs, a skittish laugh, more from embarrassment than anything else. "What's so different about me?"

"I don't know," Charles replies ponderously. "But I think there is."

Alec giggles. "You don't exactly put me at my ease do you?"

Charles shrugs, runs his hand through his hair. "You haven't changed a bit Alec. Still the perfect gentleman: tact, diplomacy, geniality. It's all over your face. It's even written on the clothes you wear.

"Now you're trying to be offensive. The others told me not to see you. He'll only be contemptuous if you go running back to him as soon as he calls, they said."

"Why did you come then?"

"I don't know. I suppose because you were a friend once, and I don't like letting friends down."

"Once a friend always a friend eh?"

Alec smiles thinly. Pause.

"Ah by the way," continues Charles. "I've invited somebody to tea. Somebody I particularly want you to meet."

"Anybody I know?"

"I should doubt it."

"Male or female?"

"Female."

"This gets more and more interesting every minute. Is she pretty?"

"I'll let you judge that for yourself."

"What does she do?"

"She's a prostitute."

"A prostitute?" exclaims Alec and then more subdued, a faint smile on his face. "Is this one of your practical jokes Charles?"

"Not at all."

Alec is stunned. He stares at Charles incredulously. He isn't sure whether Charles is having him on. "B… But, but why a prostitute?" he eventually stammers.

"Because I want you to meet her."

"A tart… My dear chap if you think… There are plenty of nice girls around."

"Don't worry you don't have to fuck her if you don't want to. I personally prefer prostitutes. So called nice girls expect you to marry them. With a prostitute there's no fuss, no emotional involvement, no responsibility and probably cheaper to boot."

"I could never go with a prostitute."

"Why?"

Alec hesitates. He is still a virgin. The subject makes him uncomfortable. "I just couldn't." he replies. A chill runs down his spine and a nervous twitch crosses his face."I just couldn't. Well damn it: you don't pay for that sort of thing."

"Saves a lot of time if you do I assure you. Just think of the time I'd waste if every time I wanted a screw I had to chase all over town for it. As it is I give this girl a ring and she's with me within the hour."

Alec shakes his head ponderously. "You're a strange fellow Charles. Most guys think they're wasting time when they're not chasing women."

"All I can say is thank God I'm not like most guys. If copulating and rearing children is the be and end all of life I'd go and stick my head in the gas oven this minute."

"I agree with you entirely Charles. It's just that, well... I couldn't go with a prostitute."

"How do you manage then?"

Alec stares at the floor. He picks his nails nervously. He is feeling acutely inadequate. Somehow Charles is getting under his skin. He wishes he had listened to the others and never come."I have a girl friend," he replies almost inaudibly.

"Platonic of course."

Alec is feeling weak. He tries to show anger by raising his voice: "I think you're being very offensive Charles. I don't want to discuss the subject any more. My personal life is my affair. I came round here because I wanted us to be friends again. Instead, you've... you've done nothing but make me feel... I don't know what. You've got absolutely no consideration for others at all."

"I'm sorry if I've hurt your susceptibilities old boy."

Pause.

"Why do you want me to meet this girl anyway?"

I'm not sure you'd like it if I told you."

"Another of your gratuitous insults I suppose.?"

"I think you'd take it that way."

"You're not going to tell me then?"

Charles scrutinizes Alec thoughtfully, then says: "If you really want to know I asked you round here because I think you can teach me something."

"Teach you something?"

Charles nods and flicks his hair out of his eye.

"From me?" Alec is really looking bewildered, as though he had been accused of stealing. His mouth is hanging open and he is staring vacuously at Charles. "I can teach you something?… You can learn something from me?… I can't imagine for the life of me what it is."

No reply. Charles's expression is like a poker face.

"Are you going to tell me what you think I can teach you?"

"I honestly think you'd be offended."

"If it's something nasty I think I can take it."

"You won't like it I assure you." Alec frowns and Charles continues: "If I tell you will you promise not to leave?"

"Is it something to do with this tart?" he asks cautiously.

Charles nods.

"Okay, I'll stay."

"Be more precise. Give me an exact time."

"You're a suspicious bastard. You really are. I've given you my word. I can't do more."

"Very well, I won't tell you what I think you can teach me."

"You said you would."

"I said nothing of the kind."

Pause.

Alec grabs his coat, stands up. "All right then; if that's how you want it I'll leave at once."

"And break your word. Surely you wouldn't do that?"

For a moment Alec is torn in indecision, riveted where he stands. Why does Charles always manage to get the better of him? Of course he can't leave now: he's given his word: a promise is sacrosanct. He slowly sits down, as though uncertain whether the bed is still there. Still nursing his coat he stares at the floor. And gradually his mood of dejection changes. He feels a strange uplift, then he even begins to feel high. It is as though a pep pill was working on him. He doesn't understand what is happening. He looks at Charles curiously, as though he is expecting him to give an answer to a silent question. Then he suddenly bursts out laughing. "You're an odd fish Charles. Really odd… I don't know why I put up with your insolence… All right I promise not to leave before six. Does that satisfy you?"

Charles nods, leans forward over the desk and runs both hands through his hair. "I'll come straight to the point." he says. "You have a quality I lack. I don't know if it can be taught, but if it can you're the one to teach me. What I'm talking about is your charm. For some reason or other, I don't know why, people like you. On the other hand with me they take an instant dislike. And God knows I've probably got a hundred more qualities than you. I'm brighter, more hard working, stronger willed, more athletic, even better looking I think. Yet, for all that, somehow or other, you leave more of an impression on people than I do. Why? I have asked myself the question a thousand times. And the only conclusion I come to is that you have that indescribable quality called charm. What it is I don't know, but you have it and I don't. From you I want to learn the art of being charming."

Alec is speechless. He gapes at Charles as though he is demented.

"You don't have to look so surprised. You wanted to know why I asked you here. Now you know."

"I don't understand," Alec falters. "I really don't. You're an enigma: the biggest question mark I've ever met."

"Nothing to understand. You have charm. I apparently don't. I want to learn what it is. If you want to know why that's a different matter, but I don't mind telling you. It's really quite simple. In life charm is a prerequisite to practically everything. You can do little without it. All great men have had it. Obviously they've had other qualities too. But it's charm that has gives them that initial break, an audience. You can't influence people, I reckon, unless in some way or other they like you or are attracted by you. What attracts them I don't know, but I think it's charm. If I hope to do anything, get anywhere in life, I'll have to cultivate the quality, appear to have it, even if I haven't really got it."

Alec gives a forced laugh. "You can't acquire charm like you do a pack of cigarettes ... Anyway, what has this to do with this prostitute you're so eager for me to meet?"

"I want you to meet Sarah for a very special reason. She's the sort of girl I imagine you wouldn't normally meet. She is an outcast, a fallen member of society, uneducated, immoral, vulgar, lazy, stupid and all the other things you've been brought up to despise. You, on the other hand, are respectable, honest, high principled: an excellent member of society. In effect you are poles apart. Her natural instinct should be to dislike you: anyway for what you stand for; if only because you will show her up for what she is. Nobody likes that. But I have a strange feeling she'll like you. That's the odd thing about you, people like you even when they shouldn't. I tried the experiment on another bloke, respectable, conventional, your type; and she couldn't stay with him more than five minutes: of course when she realized I wasn't introducing him as a prospective client… I haven't told her a thing about you Alec. In fact she doesn't know you're coming. You start from scratch and you're on your own. No help from me." He leans back in his chair grinning."That's it. My cards are on the table."

"You're diabolical," cries Alec standing up still clutching his coat. "Diabolical… You want to use me as a kind of guinea pig. It's disgusting. It really is. You have no respect for others. You use them. I'm going. Goodbye. " He moves towards the door.

"You're not going to break your word old boy?"

Silence.

Alec stands holding the door handle. He wants to go and yet feels he has to stay. He was a bloody fool to promise anything. Why had he given his word? He should have listened to the others and not come. He returns to the bed and sits down. There is a little over an hour to go: he will stick it out, then never see Charles again.

"What time is this prostitute coming?"he asks.

"She should be here any minute."

Pause.

"I can see why people don't like you. You're evil."

"You asked for the truth and I gave it to you. If you're not tough enough to take it that's your problem."

Alec is sullen again. He's desperately trying to fight off that dispirited feeling creeping through his mind and body. He doesn't want to show Charles how shaken he is. Charles despises weakness and to let anything get you down is weakness. "I'll be damned if I let myself go in front of this scoundrel." Alec says to himself. He coughs. Conflicting, strange emotions are pulling him in different directions. A tear rolls down his cheek. Fortunately, for him, however, there is a knock on the door and he is shaken out of himself. He looks up expectantly. He has never met a prostitute. He has been brought up that the better people don't frequent them.

Sarah doesn't see Alec at once. She bounces into the room

as though she knew it well. She gives Charles a peck on the cheek which he doesn't reciprocate. "Hello darling," she coos and then stops when she sees Alec."So we have company?" she says, her voice becoming more even.

Charles introduces them without getting up.

"Glad to meet you Alec I'm sure."

They shake hands and exchange how-do-you-dos. Sarah parts her full, sensual lips into a friendly smile. She is fair, with blond hair cropped short like that of a boy. Her eyes are wide and blue and when she looks at anything she stares and gives the impression of intense interest. She now fixes her eyes on Alec in this manner. He blushes a little, shifts his gaze away from hers. She looks like a tart, he thinks: too much powder, paint round the eyes, perfume; her heels are high; her skirt (under her grey coat which she has removed) is micro and red; the top part of her body is covered with a tightly fitting blue and white pullover. Her breasts stand out perkily, invitingly. She has a slender figure, medium height, with a fine waist line which accentuates her gently protruding full behind. A good looker, no doubt about that. Alec is attracted to her seductive curves as he runs his eyes over her breasts, buttocks, thighs. Then his own curiosity makes him feel guilty and he stares vacantly at the floor. She sits in an easy chair. Then her eyes again fix Alec hypnotically. He tries to look at her again, but he is aware of his lust and looks away.

"What do you think of her?" Charles breaks the silence.

"Very pretty," says Alec rapidly, quickly glancing round the room not resting his eyes on anything. A leg begins trembling. He puts the other one over it to suppress the movement. He fidgets with a shoe lace. He would like to hide under the bed.

"Alec is a gentleman," Charles is saying. "His parents are comfortable. He's been to a good school and now he's at university. What he's going to do after his degree he's not quite sure. But he'll be all right, a gentleman, anyway in this country, always is."

"Is this resumé necessary?" Alec cuts in.

"My dear chap I was only trying to break the ice. I've told you a little about Sarah. It"s only fair I should tell her something about you."

Alec doesn't reply. His lips twitch. He again shifts his legs. He is committing mental harakiri.

"He's shy." Sarah smiles affectionately. "You've no need to be shy of me dear. I'm the friendly sort you know."

"I told him what you do. No need to advertise the fact."

Sarah throws Charles an awkward look, half smiles, forces herself to laugh. "Charles is a great teaser,"she says, then turns to Alec: "Did you say you were a student dear?

"Alec nods.

"I like students: they're so clever. What subjects do you do?"

"Geography is my speciality."

"Geography. That's nice… I knew a student once who did geography. Ever so nice. Traveled all over the world he had."

"Have you been abroad?" asks Alec feeling duty bound to make some sort of conversation.

"No dear. I can't afford it. But I'd like ever so much to go to all them wonderful places. If I had money I'd travel and travel and travel. Travel is an education in itself don't you think?"

"One certainly learns a lot through travel," acknowledges Alec.

She sighs wistfully. "It must be marvelous to travel."

"Yes." Awkward pause. Then Alec forces himself to speak: "Do you like the cinema?"

"There's nothing I like more. I like them cowboys best. Them with a lot of shooting."

"I like Westerns too." Alec says genially; then after another pause adds: "How about the theater?"

"No dear. Not enough oomph on the stage. Too much talk. I like things to happen."

"A lot of action?" he supplies.

"That's right dear: a lot of action. I like a lot of action, chases and all that."

Pause. Charles is grinning. He flicks his hair back out of an eye: "That exhausts that topic of conversation. Move on to something else."

Alec throws Charles a piercing look. He is desperately searching his mind for something to say, but what can he talk about? Sarah is sitting, knees together, staring at him intently.

"Why don't you tell Alec about some of your clients. My life as a tart — the unexpurgated version."

Alec goes crimson.

"You are a teaser Charles." She smiles sweetly. She also has blushed.

Alec is staring at the floor. He nibbles the nail on his right thumb. He knows it is silly to feel so tense. The silence is painful. Every second is like an hour. All Alec's nails are short, bitten or picked. Eventually Sarah breaks the silence: "I'm sure you boys would like a cupper. A nice cupp'a tea keeps worries at sea: that's what I always say... Where's the kettle Charles? ... Oh there it is." She collects it from the floor and hurries from the room to fill it with water.

"This is positively evil," splutters Alec as soon as the door shuts.

"Don't you like her old boy? I don't think she's a bad looking bint. Nothing in the head of course, but one can't have everything."

"You're being bloody offensive again Charles. Ever since I set foot in this room you've tried to make yourself as disagreeable as possible. I don't know what has got into you."

Charles does not reply and Sarah returns and puts the kettle on his electric heater. Alec is now feeling all right again.

He is bewildered by his changes in mood. He feels Charles is playing with him, manipulating him as though he was a marionette. He sits tight, expressionless, hands folded over his lap, feet together. He doesn't want to make a fool of himself. He won't give Charles the pleasure of seeing what sort of a hold he has over him. He throws his watch a quick glance. 5.15.

"What would you boys like to eat?" says Sarah.

"There's nothing to eat," Charles replies.

"I can go and get something." She looks at Alec. "You'd like something wouldn't you dear?"

"I'm quite happy with a cup of tea thank you very much."

"There's some lovely éclairs at a little shop downstairs. They're really good. I can recommend them."

"I'll do what everybody else is doing."

"None for me," says Charles.

"But you like them so much dear."

"I don't want any today."

She is standing by the door. "I'll get an extra one in case you change your mind."

"I won't change my mind," he snaps back.

She shrugs and leaves. She has began to descend when Alec leaps up and rushes from the room. "You stay here," he tells her. "I'll get them. Just tell me where to go."

"That's all right dear. The exercise will do me good."

"Are you sure?"

She doesn't reply but her heels go clickety-click down the stairs. Alec sullenly comes back into the room and sits down.

"That little ploy didn't work did it old boy.'"

"I'll have you know Charles I'm leaving at 6:00 on the dot."

"The incredible thing about you Alec is she likes you. I've been watching you closely. You've done absolutely nothing. You've been sitting there like an embarrassed school kid. One would think you'd never seen a woman in your life. You haven't even flattered her and Sarah adores flattery. And yet she likes you. It's really hard to understand. If you were famous, a film star or something well…"

"For God's sake shut up Charles." cries Alec blocking his ears with his hands. "Don't you think I've got any feelings at all? If you want to analyze my character do it behind my back. I'm sick of your bloody opinions."

Charles grins, raises his voice. "You mustn't be so touchy old boy. I didn't mean any harm. I just want to learn from you."

"Like hell you do. You don't want to learn anything from me or anybody else. You just want to kick people around. I don't know why. Well, one thing is certain: after today I wont see you any more, ever."

Charles is eyeing Alec with a little sneer about his lips. He is not in the least troubled by the outburst. You might even get the impression he is enjoying it.

"You know something," he says. "You're not even disagreeable when you're trying to be. The thing about you Alec is you're genuinely a nice person. You don't put on an act. You really like people. Even your anger is righteous, without malice: you might almost say ineffective, as though you weren't angry at all…'"

Alec shouts: "I told you I didn't want to be analyzed to my face." His lips are quivering; he is trying to say something more, but no words come. His hands are clammy as he clenches his fists,

Charles continues: "I've always had a theory that charm and weakness go hand in hand. I'm not so sure I'm not right. People like to see the little failings of others. It gives their own ego a boost. 'I'm better than that creep' you tell yourself. He's a nice chap all the same. And why is he a nice chap? He's a nice chap simply because he makes you feel good. Take yourself for instance. I should be annoyed with you. Yet I'm not. And if I ask myself why, the answer is that your anger means nothing to me. I know perfectly well that inside you wont hurt a soul, maybe you can't: you're harmless, as harmless as a rabbit. Underneath one feels you've got no guts, no spunk. You're not a man, but a little boy in long trousers. You're frightened of growing up, showing yourself as you really are, being yourself."

Here he breaks off. Alec has his face down buried in his hands. He feels tears running down his cheeks, but he doesn't want Charles to see them. He thinks Charles is talking about his virginity.

The other pursues his line of thought relentlessly: "That's perhaps the secret of your charm. You know something: I've never heard anybody say they dislike you. 'No man who is worth his salt is all that nice'. I think it was Shaw who said that. And he's absolutely right. If a man has any spunk he's bound to tread on a few toes. You haven't an enemy in the world have you Alec? A perfectly charming, respectable, decent... Are you crying old boy?... I'm sorry, I thought you could take it. Would you like me to talk about something else?" He pauses, shrugs and goes on: "Perhaps not... Forgive me if I've offended you..."

"You bloody liar." Alec screams beside himself, standing up, tears streaming down his cheeks. "You're...you're...". He flops back on the bed and again buries his face in his hands.

A few minutes later Sarah returns holding a small parcel. Alec wipes away his tears, stifles his sobbing and gains control over himself. Sarah has noticed nothing and removes three éclairs from the package.

"I told you I didn't want one," Charles says angrily.

"I got one all the same." She smiles mischievously. "If you don't eat it, one of us will."

"Why can't you do what you're told?"

"I thought I was pleasing you."

"You know damn well you're not pleasing me. You're pleasing yourself. You're giving way to your impulses, your generous, kind impulses. Here am I trying to exercise self-restraint and you come and dangle temptation under my nose. If I'd wanted an éclair I would have said so."

Sarah gives a deep sigh. "I think you're making a lot of fuss about nothing."

"It's not nothing."

"Have it your own way dear."

"Don't speak to me like that."

She looks at him mischievously, smiles and salutes. "Sir."

"That's better. In future speak to me properly."

Her eyes are sparkling. "And supposing I don't?" She looks at him intently.

"You'll get into trouble."

"What sort of trouble?"

"Big trouble."

"How big?"

"Enormous."

"Will you punish me?" she asks merrily.

"If you misbehave or disobey me again I'll do just that."

"What will you do?"

"Something you won't like."

"What?"

"You know as well as I do."

"Will you make me go and stand in the corner?"

"More than that. Much more."

"Oh!"

She laughs. Charles doesn't. She smothers her laughter. "Am I forgiven?" she asks.

"Are you sorry? Do you promise not to disobey me again?"

"I promise. On my honor." She sulks, pouts her lips like a naughty school girl.

"Very well. Get and make the tea now. But I forbid you to have an éclair."

"But I love éclairs," she protests: "They'll only be wasted if neither of us have one. Alec can't eat three."

"Don't argue with me girl. Hurry up and make the tea."

"What will you do if I eat one?"

Charles doesn't reply at once. She quickly prepares the tea, offers a cup, together with an éclair, to Alec. The previous little scene has had a strange effect on him. He has quite forgotten his tears. He is trying to understand himself. He has his hands in his lap, the fingers over his crotch. He is trying to hide his erection. Charles is playing with him he knows.

"Before you sit down have a look in the cupboard, I've bought myself a little present."

She glances at the cupboard excitedly, nervously. "A new one?" She throws Charles a quizzical look.

He nods.

She skips over to the cupboard and as she does so accidentally knocks Charles's desk. Some tea spills, mostly on the table, but a few drops on his papers.

"Now look what you've done you careless, stupid girl."

"I'll get a cloth."

"Come here." He waits until she is by his side, next to the desk. "Now lick it up," he orders.

"You're joking Charles."

"No, I'm not."

She looks bewildered. "I won't do it," she protests.

"You'll do what I tell you."

"Not that Charles. Your table hasn't been dusted for ages."

Pause. Sarah looks from one man to the other, uncertain what to do.

"I'm waiting," says Charles.

"You're crazy," cries Alec standing up. "You can't make her lick your desk. It's disgusting… I mean the idea… It's positively revolting."

"Keep out of this. Don't meddle in things that don't concern you."

Sarah quickly comes to the rescue. She smiles at Alec. Her eyes are wide and loving. "I always do what Charles tells me. He has such a strong will. I wish I was strong like him."

"You mustn't do it," cries Alec.

"I don't mind. I really don't. I was only joking when I said I wouldn't do it." She quickly licks the tea off the desk. "There," she says standing up.

Charles wipes his finger over where she has just licked. "Once more," he tells her.

She obeys.

Alec is still standing, riveted, hypnotized. Charles scrutinizes him as though he is a liquid in a test tube. "I'm beginning to learn quite a lot about you," he says. "Feeling sexy old boy?"

Again Alec goes crimson. That is precisely how he feels. He sits down meekly.

"I have a theory about you," pursues Charles. "Well, not exactly about you. A theory relating sex and charm. I'm sure there's a connection. Tell me about your sex life Alec. What do you like doing when you're with a woman? Or what do you like her doing to you?… Come now, be honest. There's nothing to be ashamed of."

Alec doesn't reply. He feels sick, faint, as though he had received a blow in the solar plexus. His erection is gone, forgotten. He is trying to make sense of his ups and downs. What is Charles doing to him? Why is he doing it so well? How come he feels so deflated, weak, empty? It strikes him he is under a spell: Charles is hypnotizing him. The others are looking at him, he knows, coldly watching him, observing his every move and reaction. He keeps perfectly still. He wants to betray nothing. He is frightened. He doesn't know if it is of the others or himself. The silence is excruciating. He hates every second. He feels himself splitting apart. He wants to scream, scratch his eyes out, shit in his pants. Most of all he wants to forget, be away from it all. He knows he hasn't come to see Charles just out of friendship. There is something else. He has an agonizing sense of guilt.

Charles breaks the silence. "Do you want to be whipped?" he fires the question like a pistol shot.

"Whaaaaaat?" Alec manages to stammer.

"You heard."

"I... I... I. You're absolutely crazy Charles,"

"Get it out of the cupboard." He flicks a finger at Sarah.

She goes and opens the closet door and takes out a long thin cane."Oh Charles, it's a beauty," she cries excitedly.

"Give it to me."

She does so and he runs a hand along the smooth surface. He then stands up and flicks the air viciously. He does this several times. Alec is mesmerized by the swishing of the cane, the whistling of rushing air.

"What would you like?" asks Charles. "To beat or be beaten?"

No reply. Alec feels himself reddening. Then that same physical sensation, a gradual easing of his depression.

"You don't have to be shy about these thing," pursues Charles. "One should exploit ones desires not inhibit them."

"I want to go," says Alec meekly.

"Not yet old boy. I still don't know all I want to know, Besides it's not 6:00 yet."

Pause. Charles turns to Sarah. "Bare your bottom girl. Let Alec have a look at it."

She obeys without a murmur. She slips down her knickers, hose stockings and lifts up her dress.

"Bend over the chair," instructs Charles. "Stick your bottom up high."

No sooner said than done. Charles moves round his desk and holds her dress up over her back. "How's that for a behind old boy? Beautiful isn't it?"

Alec can't look. He is scarlet. He is shivering. His mind is a whirl mental masturbation. Why has Charles made him so depressed when only a minute ago he was beginning to feel all right. Charles is standing behind Sarah brandishing the cane.

"Shall I give her six of the best old boy?"

No answer.

"Come now my dear chap you went to a Public School, not me. Did you ever get the cane?… No you're not the sort. Did you enjoy beating your fags? I assume you were a prefect?"

"Stop it. Stop it. I can't stand it any longer." Alec jumps up and almost leaps towards the door. Not quite fast enough however, for Charles swivels round and in one swift movement lashes Alec's seat with all his might. Alec yelps. He stops. He gasps. For a moment his body is perfectly still, then he rushes from the room…

"Hey wait," cries Charles chasing after him. But Alec is already scrambling down the stairs. "You've forgotten your coat."

"Throw it down to me."

"No, you come and get it. You haven't even said good-bye."

Silence.

Charles goes back into his room. He leaves the door open. Alec has stopped two flights below. He doesn't want to leave without his coat. Nor does he want to go upstairs again. For a few moments he vacillates. Then slowly he begins to climb back upstairs. He lingers outside the room. He is embarrassed. He tells Charles to pass him his coat.

"You can come in you know."

Gingerly he does so. He stands just inside the room. They stare at him. His hands are clutched awkwardly in front of him. Charles is holding the coat.

"Don't take it so badly old boy. It's not the end of the world."

I hate you," hisses Alec.

"You shouldn't you know," says Charles. "We complement each other."

"My coat please."

Charles looks at his watch, holds the coat up by the shoulders, ready to slip into. But Alec grabs it and flees.

He stumbles down the stairs with a terrific clatter. Only at the bottom does he pause to put his coat on. He feels guilt and shame. Though the others said nothing he knows they have seen the dark stain in his crotch.

MONDAY NIGHT

HE IS SHORT, STOUT, GREASY. His nose is flat, his lips thick and he wears spectacles. As a kid he was called "Piggy". Now that he is middle-aged, proprietor of a night club, rich, people only say nasty things about him behind his back.

No, that's not quite true. The comedian in the club show refers to him as 'Dirty Dan', "the fat slob who greets you when you come in," Aristotle Papanzoulous, that's his name, clearly Greek, was brought over to The Bahamas when he was a baby. The club is called Dirty Dan because it seems to attract the visitors.

Every night *Aristotle* stands at the door greeting the tourists. "Good evening Madam. Good evening sir. Welcome." He bows slightly, forces himself to smile, tries to appear solicitous. The truth is the whole rigmarole makes him sick. And you can't imagine the trouble he has behind the scenes — with the Labor Office, Unions, Immigration. All because he needs to employ expatriates. Even when he can get natives to do a job they are no good and want top pay. Though, he acknowledges liking some Bahamians he thinks the majority should be back in the trees,

Nor does he get any consolation from his family. The wife is fat, bitchy, extravagant. The children are noisy, messy and lazy — pests. At least at the club he can drink. For him it's cheap. The truth is he drinks too much. The wife accuses him of being in a semi stupor all the time. No doubt true. That's the only way, he claims, he can survive.

Liquor however isn't his first love. What he enjoys more than anything is sex — preferably with clean, young Americans girls. On some nights they pour into the club. He ogles them. His mouth waters and he pours himself (or rather the barman does) a triple whisky. Ninety percent of the time these cuties are out of bounds — accompanied, in groups, something or other. The odd ten percent are either not worth bothering about or won't bother with him.

For the most part then sex is out. (he gave it up with the wife several years ago). The other big thing in his life is gambling. Once a week (every Monday when things are quiet at the club) he goes to the Casino on Paradise Island. Residents are not allowed to gamble, but he always manages to arrange something. He drinks, smokes and somebody else puts the chips on the table, all the while he keeps his eyes open for the pretty girls.

On occasion, while at the table supervising his pupil he manages to pick up a woman, usually a prostitute — not very young, not very pretty, sometimes not even American. (Beggars can't be choosers, he thinks) More often than not she has a room in a nearby hotel and they go there. It's all very discreet. He knows full well, that in his position he can't afford a scandal in a small place like Nassau. When it's all over he takes a cab back home. He's given up driving. Too dangerous, he reckons, with all the liquor he carries in his veins.

That's his weekly routine and for the most part pretty humdrum. Then one Monday night an incident occurred that he will remember for the rest of his days. As usual, when the club was quiet and he was high, but not drunk, he went to the Casino. As was normal on such occasions he wore a dark blue suit, double-breasted, expensive material and tailored to give his paunch minimum prominence. A cigar was stuck in his mouth.

Soon he had found a clean cut young man, tall, slender, (a smooth looking bloke) to play Black Jack for him. Tom Nixon was at the Casino bar downing one glass of liquor after another. Aristotle hoisted himself on the stool next to him and after a few preliminary niceties got Tom to talk about himself —a tale of woe, how he had lost a lot of money. A.P. offered him a drink and told the guy about a winning system which was almost infallible. He then suggested Tom play a few hands for him, of course, he'd reward him. "If you like my technique," he went on "we could either go Dutch or you can play for your own account and perhaps make up your losses."

After less than half an hour they were up over a thousand dollars. In the mean time Tom's wife had joined them. She was a stunner: young, neat and slender, exactly his type, the sort of woman who turned him on. Her eyes were blue; her smile was sexy with lips that looked as though she spent her day sucking sodas. She watched her husband as instructions were given. Now and again she threw Papanzoulous a mischievous glance.

This did not last long, however, for Tom decided he wanted to play for himself. A.P. protested, said he hadn't had enough experience and suggested they partner until he got a better hang of things. Tom, however, would have none of it. He instructed his wife to act on Papanzoulous's behalf at another table. She scowled, but did what she was told. A.P. followed her.

"I hate gambling," she said as soon as they were at a safe distance from her husband. "And he loves it. He's been hanging round the tables ever since we came here three days ago. Tonight I couldn't take it any more, so I went on a night club tour."

"If you are here tomorrow night you must come to my club, You are welcome as my guest. Bring whoever you want."

She smiled a thank-you and said unfortunately they were leaving the following day. Tom had an important engagement on the Wednesday morning.

A.P. then suggested if she didn't want to gamble they could have a drink together. "I would have taken you to the Casino show, but there isn't one on Mondays."'

"I saw it yesterday."

They went to the bar and found a table in a corner against the wall. He ordered himself a double Scotch and Corinna (that was her name) had a Coke.

"I hope your husband wins." he said. "When I met him he had lost rather a lot and was very depressed."

"He always loses." Then she told him how mean he was. Even when he won he never gave her a penny, though he was loaded, having inherited most of his money.

He took a gulp at his whisky. He had been drinking steadily the whole evening and felt good.

Soon more drinks were ordered. Then more again. Corinna guzzled Coke like an addict. She didn't stop talking. He got the impression she was stoned. She was warm and friendly, bleary eyed. He couldn't take his eyes off her. Then he thought he wasn't hearing straight. She was quite casually suggesting she take him to her room. She dismissed reference to her husband with a little sniff of her nostrils. She said he would be at the tables for hours.

The next thing he knew he was in a hotel room. She locked the door, dimmed the lights, found some soft music on the radio. She told him to make himself comfortable. Then came the first blow, She wanted money. She carefully explained she wasn't a prostitute. She was just cash short. A.P. couldn't be bothered to argue, so he gave her two hundred dollars, double the standard rate.

"I want another hundred," she said.

What the hell, he thought. He'd just won a pile. He fancied her. She was his type. The professionals he had seen roaming the Casino weren't a patch on her. He gave her the money. Things then went rather well for him. She stripped, did a little show and after that slowly undressed him. She was great, he thought. She really made him feel good. He felt he was floating on a cloud. "My lucky day," he thought. Soon they were on the bed. And that's when he got his second shock. Too much Scotch? Desire in the head but not where he wanted it? In short he couldn't perform. He felt fine, however. He was convinced he wasn't drunk, after all he was used to heavy drinking. He got down on the floor and did a few press-ups. He told her he would be all right in a moment. But Corinna wasn't impressed and began dressing. He protested, grabbing her. It wasn't just the money, he felt. His pride and manhood were at stake.

"I'll give you another hundred bucks," he said.

She laughed.

"Two hundred."

She laughed some more.

"How much do you want?'"

"I don't want anything. I want a man."

Reluctantly he began to put his clothes on. `She was a bitch', he thought ` No point arguing'. However, he didn't feel too bad: all his life he had been made fun of and he was sort of used to it, though not entirely. He consoled himself that for a short time she had made him feel good, really good. He straightened his tie, tied the laces on his shoes, stood up. Then ,just as he was going to give her a final good-bye peck the door handle turned.

"Christ." Corinna groaned in a hushed whisper, "That must be Tom. He'll kill you if he finds you here."

"I'll hide in the cupboard."

"No. There." She pointed to the window. "Hurry, he's got a gun. Don't try any funny business." She dashed into the bathroom and called to Tom that she was just coming.

He slipped out of the window. His glasses fell off. All he could see was darkness as he clung to the outer sill. Slowly he lowered himself, his toes groping along the wall. He looked down, but it was pitch black. He was terrified of falling. He prayed for some quick thinking from Corinna. Maybe she would persuade Tom back to the tables, or to the bathroom, something anyway.

He could hear snippets of talk in loud shrill voices. Tom was rasping. "Where is that fat slob?" "Why was the door locked?" She replied: "I didn't realize I'd bolted it. And I was in the bathroom. There was a drip and I couldn't stop it." A.P. waited anxiously. He hoped she would come and rescue him from his precarious position.

But it wasn't Corinna who came to the window, but Tom. In fear the old man slipped a notch, but was relieved that his toes found something solid—a ledge, he imagined. Anyway, he was thankful that some of the weight was off his hands and wrists.

"Well, well, well," said Tom, a nasty smirk about his lips. "If it isn't my friend Fatso. Are you coming or going?"

"Help me up."

"This isn't your room Fatso. What do you want to come in for?"

No reply.

Tom leered at him a few moments. Then, after a long pause he broke the silence: "Has anybody told you Fatso that you are extraordinarily ugly? You have one of the most repulsive faces I've ever seen." He tweaked the helpless man's cheeks and twisted his nose.

Papanzoulous tried to bite him.

"Ah, naughty, naughty." Then Tom turned away and called his wife: "Darling, our fat friend here is hungry. Will you get some soap from the bathroom."

Very shortly the old Greek was coughing and spluttering as suds were pushed down his nostrils and bits of soap were rammed in his mouth.

"Still hungry Fatso?"

Papanzoulous shook his head and sneezed. He continued to sneeze at various intervals. All the while being tormented. Tom said the gambling system was no good: he had lost. Then he leisurely removed the old man's wallet from his inside pocket and went through its contents. He fished out a bundle of cards.

"Aristotle Papanzoulous," he read from one of them. Then went on. "Oh, what's this? You didn't tell me you had another name. It's far more appropriate I think. Your illustrious ancestor would shudder in his grave if he knew you bore his name. Do you mind if I just call you Dirty Dan, or is that too intimate?"

No answer.

He counted the money in the wallet and then pocketed it.

"I paid your wife," said the other.

"What did you pay her for Dirty Dan? On second thoughts do you mind if I call you Dirty Dick? I prefer it.' When there was silence he called to Corinna. "Darling, what did he pay you for?"

'He didn't pay me nothing," she screeched.

He looked back at his victim, flaring in mock anger, waving his forefinger as though he had been a troublesome little boy. "You've been lying to me Dirty Dick. That's very wicked. I must teach you a lesson." His head vanished for an instant.

The next thing A.P. felt was pain. The younger man had removed a shoe and with the heel began wacking the knuckles in front of him. He went about it methodically, rhythmically, with varying force, as though he was playing a Xylophone.

"Stop. Please stop," begged the old man.

Tom merely whistled and continued to wham the knuckles in time with the beat of his tune. He went on playing this barbarous game for several minutes. Fortunately for Papanzoulous he only needed his hands to keep his balance and not support his weight. If he had fallen and been hurt , perhaps killed, didn't seem to worry Tom at all. Then, for no apparent reason the wacking stopped.

"This is what I think of liars." said Tom in feigned disgust and spat in the victim's face, He watched the slobber slither down the fat nose and cheeks.

"You're a filthy bastard," cried the other.

Tom took out his gun and aimed it at the old man. "Now don't you go calling me names. Say you're sorry."

"Sorry".

His hands and fingers were smarting; his arms were aching; ditto his toes. How long had he been in this ridiculous position, he wondered? It seemed for ever. All he knew is he mustn't let go.

"I don"t like the way you say sorry. I'm not convinced you mean it. You'll. have to do better than that." Tom put his foot on the sill, so that it jutted over the edge. "Lick the sole of my shoe," he said.

Painfully the old man hauled himself up and did what was asked. He was grimacing.

"So you think it's dirty do you? Never mind. I'll wash you clean." He put his pistol in his pocket and took out another one. The Greek was horrified. He shut his eyes tightly and lowered his head. The next thing he felt was a jet of warm liquid over his hair, down his cheeks and chin.

The humiliations that followed are too repulsive to repeat. Tom had no mercy. It struck A.P. he might be murdered: all it required was a little push. The Bahamian CID do a fair job catching criminals, but if Tom and Corinna took the first flight out in the morning, they probably could melt away into the amorphous masses of the United States without a trace.

But it seemed Tom wasn't a killer, for after a while he stopped his games. "That'll teach you to meddle with my wife," he said. And turning away told Corinna to clean up the mess. She poured water over the face in the dark, dabbed it with a towel, combed the hair and sprayed the hands with deodorant. All the while a voice whispered in the background.

The next thing Papanzoulous knew was that he was being grabbed from behind and jerked backwards. As he fell he screamed. An instant later, as he lay on the ground, the truth dawned on him: he had been standing on a ledge above a mound no more than two feet from the ground. If he hadn't been drunk or so expectant of his amatory embrace, he would have remembered this particular lie of the land (which he knew well) and that they had only gone up one floor.

The Nixons were at the window. "He tried to break in," said Tom shrilly.

A light was beamed on the man on the ground.

"Mr. Papanzoulous," said a deep voice. "You're under arrest. The charge is attempted breaking and entering."

A.P. struggled to his feet brushing the dirt from his trousers.

"I can explain everything," he said in a cool dignified manner.

"I must warn you anything you say may be used in evidence against you."

"She's a prostitute," accused the old man.

Tom protested. He said the accusation was absurd. Corinna was his wife. He had plenty of money. To prove his point he waved the notes he had taken from the wallet. "Why would my wife want to prostitute herself when I've got all this?"

"That's my money," cried A.P. "He stole it off me."

"That's not true officer. If I'd taken the money I wouldn't be silly enough to call the police."

"I think you'd better all come down to the Station," said the deep voice.

A pang of fear shot through the Greek. An appearance in court didn't appeal to him at all. He'd have to admit to gambling, consorting with a prostitute, being drunk, otherwise the charge of attempted breaking and entering might stick.

However you looked at it, he wasn't in a happy predicament. He was a foreigner in the Bahamas and could be deported for any paltry reason. And even if he wasn't the authorities might force him to close the Club. He reckoned the bastards would be only too pleased to take it over.

"If the charges against me are dropped I'll withdraw mine against the Nixons."

Tom expostulated: "He's got nothing against us officer.'"

"Come Mr. Papanzoulous. "An arm was grabbed and he was brusquely escorted to a waiting car. Handcuffs were slipped over his wrists and he was pushed inside.

Dawn was beginning to break and for the first time Papanzoulous got a proper glimpse of the two constables. He knew the man with the gruff voice. Corporal Thompson was a big, black, burly man, a womanizer and known for his dislike of whites. Once he had caused trouble at the club trying to get a job for one of his girl friends. She was no good and A.P. fired her. The case was reported to the Labor Office and that had been a lot of bother. The whole business only fizzled out when she was paid $100.

The other policeman was tall, lean, muscular, also very black. He was the junior of the two. And though Papanzoulous had seen him around he didn't know him. They both now got in the car. The junior officer drove round to the front of the hotel and picked up the Nixons.

A.P. was trying to collect his thoughts. Thompson was between him and Corinna. The officer tried to put a hand on her thigh but she brushed it aside.

After a little while it dawned on Papanzoulous that they weren't going into town at all.

"Where are you taking us." he said trying to conceal the fear in his voice."

"SHUT UP."

Then it struck him what was happening. He made a quick decision: "Whatever Nixon has offered you I'll double it."

Thompson laughed loudly.

"Aren't we going to the Station?" said Corinna.

"Sure," came the reassuring reply.

Papanzoulous slumped back into the seat resigned. He knew what was going to happen. Ten minutes later they arrived at a deserted beach. "I'll give you triple what he offered you," he said in desperation.

"You ain't got it man." Thompson guffawed and grabbing him, pushed him out of the car onto the sand. Tom told Corinna to get out. A little hesitantly she did so. "What are you going to do?" she asked.

"Nothing dear. Just watch."

"Don't you think Tom he's had enough?"

He didn't reply, but with a nod of his head signaled Thompson. The burly policeman seized Corinna and thrusting himself against her began pulling her dress off. She screamed and lashed out.

"Stop it," cried Tom. "Deal with him first."

But Thompson didn't hear, or didn't want to hear, for in a moment he had her on the ground with her dress over her head, her knickers round her ankles. He unzipped himself.

"Help me Tom.'"

He said nothing, did nothing. She yelled, kicked, clawed, The policeman shoved, heaved, groaned. Together with the other two Papanzoulous looked on. Soon it was all over. She lay back in the sand whimpering,

"That'll teach you to go messing around behind my back you little bitch," said Tom venomously staring down at her.

"You bastard," she cried and tried to grab one of her husband's ankles.

Nimbly he moved aside. He told her she needn't bother getting up. It was only half time. He signaled the Lance Corporal. Then pointed to Papanzoulous. "Now deal with him."

"That will be my pleasure," said Thompson who was respectable again.

He punched the Greek in the stomach, kicked and trod on him, rammed a boot in his face. The others joined in the beating until eventually the old man lost consciousness.

When he came to a little while later, he was alone on the beach. His head was splitting. He was bruised and aching all over. Here and there, there were patches of blood. For a while he lay still, but then the heat of the sun began to beat down on him and he knew, if he didn't want sun-stroke, he would have to force himself up.

He staggered towards the water and fully dressed let the waves wash over him. The salt stung, but the cool refreshed. Soon he was able to shuffle up to the road and after a short wait was picked up and taken to the hospital. Later, when questioned, he said he had been attacked by hooligans and dumped. No, he didn't think he'd be able to recognize any of them, he said.

So much for what happened that famous Monday and part of Tuesday morning. The only consolation he had was that Tom was caught with his revolver when leaving the country. No doubt he would have some questions to answer, though it was doubtful if they would amount to much. Besides, he thought, that was poor consolation for what he had endured.

"Hell, what am I moaning about?" he said to himself. "It's all my own damn fault. If I didn't like drinking, gambling , screwing it wouldn't have happened. But I do." The pattern of his life is still the same. He still drinks too much, goes to the Casino every Monday night, keeps his eyes open for a pretty girl. Papanzoulous is still Papanzoulous.

THE DAY OF JUDGMENT

STAND AND STARE AT THE sky on any major street in a large city and in a few moments a little crowd will have gathered around you, also gaping upwards. People line up at bus stops, movies, immigration. During the Nazi era they even lined up to be gassed. As I walk around, brooding, thinking or doing nothing in particular I get the impression that everybody around me is dead. I see these long pale faces, mask-like with dull beady eyes. Sometimes I wonder if it's not me that's dead and the lifeless part in me that sees death everywhere I look. That was a possibility until recently. Now I know differently. The fact is everybody is dead, me included. This is confirmed (and I haven't a shadow of doubt I'm right) by the special circumstances I find myself in. You see I have just been born. The guillotine has fallen and my head has rolled into the basket.

* * * * *

"You are wanted by his Lordship," says a voice with a ring of authority.

Though it is the middle of the night or to be more precise early morning I get up without a moments hesitation. I throw some clothes on, the ones that are there ready for me and go out. I don't know the area at all. It looks like nothing I've ever seen before. The air is moist and every now and again I seem to hear a foghorn, very faint in the distance. But it could be a trumpet or some other musical instrument or simply my imagination. No matter. I walk as though I know where I'm going. After a while I come to what I think is a road and begin to cross. I am immediately seized by a firm hand on my shoulder and instructed to wait for the sign.

"What sign?" I ask.

"The one that says WALK."

"I can't see any WALK sign."

"Of course you can't. It's not on yet. Don't try and be clever."

I wait. I vacantly look around. I can't see any lights at all, let alone a WALK sign. In fact I'm not even sure the road is there now. I still feel the hand however.

"Nice day," I say to make conversation.

He doesn't answer.

"Can you tell me where I am?"

"You can go now," he says. "And when you reach the other side of the road you'll be on the other side of the road."

I deferentially cock my hat, but as I do so a gust of wind catches and blows it away. I want to chase after it, but I don't know which way it went and to be quite honest I'm not sure whether I had a hat in the first place. Boldly I walk out into the middle of the road, or at least where I think the middle of the road should be. There is a terrific clutter of hoofs and the next thing I know is I'm gathered up by the collar of my coat and hurtled through space. And very soon, just as rudely as I was collected, I am suddenly dumped. "YOU'RE HERE," I'm told.

I pick myself up and look around. Through the mist I see the stern of a ship. It is quite still and very white. Then I realize it isn't a boat at all, but as I can't describe it, I might as well stick to calling it a ship. Certainly the sea is nearby. I can hear its swish and roar as it thrashes the coastline, rocks and all that. An elevator is waiting for me and I go in. Now it dawns on me why I have come. It was silly of me not to have thought of it before. I'm referring to the interview. It stands to reason you don't get anywhere without first having an interview.

Who is going to interview me, I wonder. Maybe the Almighty himself, I think? Then it strikes me that I have never been a particularly exalted personality, so there is no reason He should put himself out.

I notice there are two others in the elevator. They are very tall and wear grey overcoats and trilby hats that hide their faces. They ignore me completely, but when the lift starts moving they begin pounding the man between them, whom I hadn't noticed. I don't in fact see him even now. I just hear his groans and sighs, the thumps and bangs, until eventually I hear a choking sound of somebody being sick. This is followed by a thud and silence. Naturally, all this is none of my business and I act as though I have seen and heard nothing, which of course is the sensible approach as I could quite obviously be hallucinating.

I was going to say that the incident made me feel a little uneasy. But that's not true. Somehow, everything seems just right, like the hand stopping me before the WALK sign and the efficient way I had been delivered to the boat, or whatever it is.

The two men (and maybe the third) got out on the eighth floor. I get out on the ninth. I am immediately struck by a holy presence, as though I'm in a room of computers, the temperature and atmospheric pressure just right. Nor is there too much light. Just enough to know what is there without seeing it. It seems that I'm expected, for a man in black is waiting for me, his back facing me. I think it rude to move round and look at his face, so I simply stand behind him and wait. He is silent. Nor does he move. I toy with the idea of prodding him, but then think better of it, in case He is God or something.

"Are you going to interview me?" I ask after a little while.

Silence.

The room is circular with windows on all sides. The carpeting is brown and here and there the room is partitioned off into little cubicles. In each cubicle there is a table and chair, also brown, but otherwise quite bare. Interview cells? But who is going to interview me, I wonder? Then where is everybody? Why am I and this black figure the only bodies around? It strikes me that I'm being tested. But tested for what? What have I done? Oh yes, I've been guillotined because I was an aristocrat instead of a peasant. Or was it a communist instead of a capitalist? Or a Jew instead of an Aryan?. I can't even begin to remember all the things I've been and done. Does he remain silent to give me time to contemplate my sins? Well, whatever I've done I've done or not done I can't change anything now. Or can I?

"How long are you going to keep me waiting?"

No reply.

"If you don't want me can I go?"

"Where do you want to go?" The voice comes from behind me and is high pitched, like a woman's, though it's a man. At least he's dressed like a male and looks like one. He's bald, fat and greasy. He wears a spotlessly white doctor's tunic and stares at me with a syrupy smile.

I am now facing him. "Who are you?" I ask.

He grins a little more, but says nothing. He is now three feet away and I can smell his meaty odor. I'm about to say something else, but before I have time to say whatever it was I was going to say another man appears. He wears shorts, T-shirt, sandals. Certainly not the right sort of dress to confront his maker or anyway his betters. He doesn't even look at us. He simply exits at the other side of the room.

"Go. Check and see if he's got any money?" says the fat greasy man.

"Who are you that I should obey you?"

"Hurry. Don't waste time. He may vanish and then you won't be able to find him."

I rush to the glass exit, which is actually a window. I immediately find myself on a kind of deck. The boards are very clean. The man isn't around. Has he gone up or down? I run to some steps that go both ways and after a moment's hesitation make a quick decision to go down. On the lower deck there seem to be hundreds of vacationers. They wear breezy colored shirts and trousers, straw and cloth hats. The man I am meant to be following looks very much like any of the other men around.

"Where has he gone?" I vaguely address three or four people.

"Where has who gone?" replies a plump middle-aged woman.

"Didn't a man come this way?"

They look at each other vacantly.

"What did he look like?"

"It doesn't matter. If you didn't see him there's not much point describing him."

Why I go down another flight of steps I don't know. As I stumble down I accidentally knock a box of keys over. There are thousands of keys, every conceivable size, shape and type. The steps are strewn with them and many fall into the sea.

"Pick them up," commands one of the vacationers.

"I haven't time."

"What do you mean you haven't time? What's the hurry?"

"I've got to find somebody."

"Are you the man whose looking for a man he doesn't know?" he asks squinting at me suspiciously.

"Leave me be," I protest.

He picks up a key and holding it up high between thumb and forefinger delicately lets it drop overboard. "GO GET IT," he cries as though he is throwing a bone to a dog and he gives me a little push. "THERE. THERE, YOU IDIOT," he points to a solitary man who is on the deck below sitting on a diving board with his feet dangling over the edge.

It is my man. "Thanks,"I yell and scamper down the few remaining steps to the deck below. What am I meant to ask him? I'm seized with panic. I suddenly realize he might kill me and there will be no witnesses. How will anybody know I've been murdered as opposed to just falling into the sea? The thought troubles me, so I climb the steps to the upper deck again. If I have some witnesses, I say to myself, he won't dare push me overboard. All I want is a few vacationers, but for some unknown reason they all scamper down from where I have just come up. They are a terribly noisy crowd, yelling, clapping, shoving each other, transistors round their necks blaring. I feel as though I'm caught in a stampede. Then an instant later they have all vanished and there is silence.

Of course I know that killing the man whom I am meant to ask a question (whatever it is) would be an accident. But how will I explain it? I have to do the explaining, not them. Besides, I'm still here. They've gone. Slowly I climb the two flights of stairs to the computer room. When I reach it only the two thugs whom I had seen in the elevator are there.

"Where's the boss?"

"He's not here."

"Where is he?"

"I don't know."

"I'll wait."

"No point. He's not coming back."

"How do you know?

The man who has done the talking up to now looks at his colleague and shrugs. Then he takes a pace towards me. I take a pace back.

"Won't you come to the elevator?" he invites.

For a moment I'm paralyzed. Then I scream "NO", and begin running. I hop on tables and chairs, but somehow everywhere I happen to be one of the thugs is standing in front of me. Eventually, my only escape is through the elevator door. I rush through it and quickly press a button. But not quick enough. A moment later I feel myself wedged between two huge bodies and.

TOMMY'S ADVENTURES IN HIS SEARCH FOR HAPPINESS

A Fable

"Mum, where shall I find happiness?" asked the little boy one day.

"Happiness darling is within you. Seek and ye shall find," she said.

Mrs. Hutton was an ordinary English housewife in her early thirties. She was a mouse of a woman, skinny, dark, long faced. She didn't take much trouble over herself and her clothes were utilitarian rather than fashionable. Nevertheless you couldn't help liking her. She was kind, quite hard working and always did her best in the things she thought mattered. The house was clean, though not too tidy; her cooking was good and she took a great deal of trouble over the children. She had three in all: two girls and Tommy. She doted over them and was prepared to suffer any hardship for their sakes. They gave her life purpose.

Tommy was the eldest. Fair, with a mop of curly hair he was nearly as tall as his mother. His face had a bright open air about it — the eyes were light blue, mercurial; the nose long and thin; the forehead high, but well balanced by a determined little chin. Tommy was always busy— making things, playing games, teasing his sisters, pestering his mother. Sometimes he worked, but not more so than the other boys his age. He seemed, to all outward appearances, perfectly commonplace. To Mrs Hutton, however, he was no ordinary little boy: he was the apple of her eye.

Many a mother is apt to think her child exceptional in some way or other and in this respect Mrs Hutton was like most mothers. She differed from them, however, in one essential: whereas most mothers are quite wrong in the judgment of their children, she was quite right in hers. Tommy was no ordinary little boy. Unlike other children he possessed a quality, which although not rare, is rare when found in an extreme degree. In the past (and history bears this out) men possessed of this quality have towered over their fellows, or, which is probably more often the case, have ended their lives in ignoniminy or on the gallows. This quality is curiosity. But not the curiosity of inquisitiveness — the prying into other peoples' affairs, or as it is more commonly called 'idle curiosity'. It is something far more noble than that: It is curiosity in the sense of scrupulousness, accuracy and the desire to know things in their beginnings. Tommy Hutton was born with such a curiosity. He believed nothing without adequate verification. And so it was no wonder that (taking the words of his mother rather too literally) he changed his personality overnight. Instead of playing, teasing, pestering (sometimes working), doing all the other wonderful things little boys do, he became passive, silent, contemplative.

"Darling what are you thinking about?" His mother asked him next day.

No answer.

"Why don't you speak to me? In anything wrong? Are you ill?'"

Silence.

"Why don't you go out and play like all the other little boys? It's not good for you to stay in all day doing nothing and all by yourself." She gave a worried frown: "You're not even listening to me. This is not like you at all. Tell me if you are not feeling well. Is there something you're frightened to tell me? Have you done something wrong? Please, please answer me."

No reply.

"Oh my poor darling you must be very very ill. I'll let your father know at once. It must be serious. No, no, I'd better phone the doctor first. You wait here while I ring. I won't be a moment." And she rushed from the room leaving Tommy deep in meditation.

The doctor came and went. Other doctors came and went. Months passed and still Tommy didn't change. The Huttons grew desperate, but there was nothing they could do. It seemed that their son would never alter. In this, however, they were mistaken, for exactly a year after his mysterious transformation he became his old self again. The family rejoiced and Mrs Hutton thanked God that all her troubles were over. But they weren't, for a few days later Tommy confronted her with a ticklish question.

"Mum, what you told me isn't true." he said,

"Quite possibly dear. I've got a lot on my mind and I don't always know what I say. What did I tell you?"

"You said I'd find happiness within me. I didn't. I found only misery. I searched and searched and the more I searched the more wretched I became. I've never been so unhappy in all my life. Mum, you showed me where to find misery, not happiness."

Mrs Hutton remembered and as she remembered she understood. She took Tommy in her arms and kissed him: "0h darling, darling all this is a terrible mistake — a dreadful misunderstanding that should never have happened. I didn't mean what you thought I meant. I meant something completely different. Yes, I know I said happiness is within you and so it is, but pursue it and it will elude you. You can't chase it like you chase a ball. The kingdom of happiness cannot be taken by storm. You enter it by accident when you are probably going somewhere else. To find it is always a surprise."

Pause.

Tommy reflected and then asked sadly: "How then shall I find happiness?"

She smiled and gave him another kiss. "Don't think about it dear. Work hard, play hard, have fun with your friends and you'll be happy. Happiness is a by-product of activity. When you're busy you haven't time to ask yourself if you're miserable: it's then that you're happy. You mark my words, the best recipe for happiness in occupation."

So Tommy set about doing what his mother advised. He worked hard, played hard and tried to have fun with his friends. He was very much like his old self, so much so that Mrs Hutton believed he had found happiness. And a few months later, feeling very certain about it, she put the question direct to him: "Are you happy dear?" she asked at breakfast one morning.

He hesitated, then shaking his head replied glumly: "No mum, I'm not happy. I don't see how I can be. What you told so isn't true. I work; I play; I try and have fun with my friends. I've done my best to keep busy and do all the things you said. But it's no good: things just don't work out that way. I keep saying to myself 'Tommy you're only trying to keep busy so as to forget how unhappy you are. You're running away from something. You're trying to drown your worries with activity.'" He stopped abruptly and giving his mother a quizzical look asked: "Mum, how can I keep busy if my heart isn't behind what I do?"

She smiled pleasantly: "You'll have to find out what your heart wants to do won't you dear?"

"How do I do that?"

"Oh darling you do ask awkward questions. At your age

you oughtn't to be tying yourself up into such knots. Why don't you get on with your cornflakes like a good boy now? You'll have plenty of time to ask difficult questions when you're a little older."

"Won't you answer my question then mum?"

Silence.

"Why don't you answer me mum?"

Mrs Hutton did not reply immediately and when she did there 'was a note of irritation in her voice, "I can't, that's why. I've told you all I know. If you want to know more you'll have to ask somebody far cleverer than me."

So Mrs Hutton took Tommy to see a psychiatrist. "This gentleman will answer all the questions you want to know," she said before leaving him.

The psychiatrist was below average height and about sixty. He had a huge dome of a forehead, large black spectacles on a big nose, thinning gray hair, plump veined cheeks that gave him a passionate look. He asked Tommy to lie on the couch.

"Well young man," he began, "Your mother tells me you have a passion for asking questions. Is that so?,"

"No,"said Tommy. "I only ask mother one question, but as she never gives me the right answer I keep asking it."

"What is the question? Perhaps I'll be able to answer it?'"

"I don't think you'd want to even if you could."

"Oh why not?"'said the psychiatrist surprised.

"Because if you did I wouldn't have to come back and see you anymore and you'd be out of a job.'"

"I want you to get better.'"

"I'm not ill."

"Your mother thinks you are. She says you're not like all the other boys your age.'"

"I don't want to be. I think they're silly.'"

"And why do you think the other boys silly Tommy?"'asked the psychiatrist gently.

"Because I'm bright and I recognize fools when I see them."

"Isn't that rather a presumptuous remark to make? What right have you to assume you're better than your friends?'"

"None, except that I believe I am."

"Why do you believe that? Have you evidence of the fact? Do you do better at work than they do? Are you better at games than they are?" He paused, but when Tommy remained silent went on: "I do not remind you of all this to discourage you, but only so that you should see yourself as you really are. Your passion for asking questions is your way of evading the responsibilities you have to face. It in my job, not so much to answer your questions, but to remove the underlying causes which prompt you to ask them in the first place. When I've done that you'll find yourself with more energy to do exactly the same as the other boys your age."

"Oho, so that's it?" cried Tommy sitting up indignantly. "You want to stop me asking questions so I'll be like everybody else. But pray tell me how will I learn anything unless I ask questions?"

The psychiatrist reflected a moment then replied: "There are two types of question—answerable ones and unanswerable. To the first category belong such questions as 'how are scrambled eggs made?' 'what is the time?' 'why is it dark at night?' and so on. The second type of question is metaphysical and usually unanswerable: 'why do I live?' 'does immortality exist?' 'Is there a God?' and similar questions. The sick mind always asks the unanswerable sort of questions."

"That's absolute nonsense,"protested Tommy. "All questions are unanswerable until they've been answered. If some people hadn't asked unanswerable questions we wouldn't know all the things we do know, would we now? How do you distinguish between your two types of question?"

"I won't answer that," replied the psychiatrist calmly. "As I have just said my job is not to answer your questions, but to help you understand why you ask them. Now tell me about your first memories "'

"Pshaw", cried the boy. "What good will that do me?"

"Plenty," said the man, "but I'm not going to be dragged into any of your discussions. Come along now, try and cooperate."

No reply.

"It's for your own good. I don't want to see you like this forever."

Tommy then asked if he could ask just one question.

"What is it?"said the psychiatrist a little irritably.

"Are you happy?"

"Er…or.Of course I'm happy. Anyway as happy an most people."

"Aha. Precisely. That's exactly what I thought," cried Tommy triumphantly. "You're no more competent to answer my question than anybody else. In fact you're like everybody else and consequently the best you can do is to make me the same. Well, that isn't what I want. I want happiness and as you can't tell me where to find it you're no good to me." Tommy jumped to his feet and nimbly darted towards the door. "Good-bye now. Thanks for nothing," and the poor psychiatrist was left alone quite bewildered.

Tommy next took to reading. He read anything and everything and much to his parents consternation would do little else. At first he started every new book with a pang of expectation for he really hoped to discover the secret for which he yearned. In this, however, he was doomed to disappointment. He read and read, but the more he read the greater became his disillusionment. Two years passed and at the end of them he was no happier. He began to doubt whether he would ever be happy. His imagination conjured up pictures of perpetual misery. At night he tossed and turned and had terrible nightmares. He grew desperate, most terribly in despair and would no doubt have eventually killed himself if he hadn't one night been awakened by a strange voice.

"Houkisboukismaloukis!   Houkisboukismaloukist! Houkisboukismaloukis!"

Tommy reached for the light but it wasn't there.

"Houkisboukismaloukis!   Houkisboukismaloukis! Houkisboukismaloukis!," the voice continued to chant melodiously.

"Oh for goodness sake, shut up," cried the boy. "How do you expect me to go to sleep if you go on with all that hooky-booky stuff?"

"Houkisboukismaloukis! Houkisboukismaloukis!" the voice went on unperturbed.

Tommy tossed and turned as though in some terrible agony, but although he tried he could not sleep. Eventually he resigned himself to circumstances, and sitting up in bed, started to ask questions: "Tell me Mr Hooky," he began "do you know where I can find happiness?"

"No," replied the voice, "but if you obey me you will find it."

Tommy laughed. "Oh come now Mr Hooky. That doesn't make sense. If you don't know where I can find it why should I obey you?"

"Houkisboukismaloukis."

"No, no, that's not good enough," snapped Tommy impatiently. "You're evading the issue. I want an answer to my question. Do you or do you not know where I can find happiness?"

"I know how you can find it, but not where," said the voice calmly.

Tommy snorted. "What sort of reply Is that?" Then he modified his tone when he realized he was asking a favor. "Please Mr Hooky can you tell me how to find happiness?"

"You don't deserve it."

"Please, I beg you sir."

There was a long pause. Then he replied: "If you want happiness you must search for it."

"But… but," choked Tommy controlling his frustration; "that's what I've been doing all my life."

"Not at all," Hooky spoke authoritatively like an Oxford don. "You have never searched for it. You have waited for it to come to you, as though it was your birthright. You have never been captain of your ship. You have let it sail hither and thither, haphazardly with each change of fortune. If you want happiness you must navigate your own ship. Be at the helm. Do your own steering. There are no two ways about it."

"Yes, yes," snapped Tommy. "That's all very well, but you don't tell me where to go."

"That's not the point. The important thing is to go. The routes are many. It is up to you to find the one which suits you best."

The boy shrugged. Then asked listlessly: "What shall I do?"

Houkisboukismaloukis," cried the voice enthusiastically.

"Yes, but can't you be a little more specific? You're vague enough as it is without all this hooky-booky stuff. Just tell me what to do."

Mr Hooky reflected a moment and then replied: "The best thing you can do now is to give up reading. Put your tomes aside: books can teach you no more than what you already take to them, and intellectual tasting of life is no substitute for experience." He paused and then continued: "Now is the time for action. Go out into the world and live: do and dare, experiment with yourself; take chances and make mistakes. Only by failing and learning where you have failed will you learn. The courage to do what you want is the only road to happiness. Take it. Houkisboukismaloukis!"

There was no reply as by this time the boy was sound asleep. Nevertheless Mr Hooky's advice must have made some impression, because a few mornings later Tommy got up very early and leaving his parents a brief good-bye note set out in search of happiness. The only thing he took with him was his cosh[1] and with it he went straight to the house of the greatest living philosopher.

"I want to see Setarcos," he said to the hag who opened the door to him.

"Setarcos is asleep," replied the woman.

"Wake him up then. I've got an important question to ask him."

"Setarcos is a great philosopher and like all great philosophers never answers questions but only asks them."

Tommy took out his cosh and waved it menacingly at the hag. "Do what I say. Fetch me Setarcos."

The hag cringed. "I will do what I can." And she hurried into the house.

A moment later she returned. "Setarcos is dead," she announced.

"Nonsense," expostulated Tommy. "I don't believe you. Let me in and I will find him." And so saying he barged his way past the hag and into the house. "Where is he? Where is he?" he cried.

He went through all the rooms but didn't find Setarcos. "Where is he?" he turned on the hag threateningly. "Bring him to me at once or I shall whack you."

The woman fell to her knees. "Spare me gentle sir."

"Only if you bring him to me at once."

There was a pause. The hag stood up. She faced Tommy squarely, her head high, her chins jutting out, her eyes popping. The stomach protruded and the breasts sagged. "I am Setarcos," she said pompously.

Tommy's jaw dropped. "But you are a woman," he gasped.

---

1   A sort of small billy club

"Your senses do not deceive you young man." Then she asked what she could to for him.

"Where can I find happiness?" he asked.

The woman gave him an odd look and promptly stood on her head.

Tommy gaped. "Why on earth are you doing that?"

"So the blood will go to my head and I will think better."

For a few moments there was silence and then Setarcos asked Tommy why he wanted happiness.

"Because I'm unhappy of course. Silly question. I thought philosophers were meant to be bright."

The hag did some leg exercises.

"Answer me," snapped Tommy; "otherwise I'll biff you."

"You're a very lucky man," said the woman hurriedly. "You see if you weren't unhappy you'd have nothing to look forward to and life wouldn't be worth living. Man lives by his hopes and illusions, so not to have any is very serious indeed. Be thankful you are as you are and there's still hope for you."

The hag jumped to her feet.

Tommy brandished his cosh aggressively. "Bah!. What sort of a reply is that? You've told me absolutely nothing and that's not what I came here to see you for. I want happiness and I want you to tell me where to find it. Is that clear?"

"Oh yes, quite."

"Go ahead then, I'm waiting." He stood feet akimbo, hands on hips,

The hag again stood on her head. She began immediately: "Happiness is the illusion by which mankind survives: it is the drug that keeps the human race going; every man, woman and child believes that within him there is a last chamber, a final closet, which when opened will bring him true and eternal happiness. It is this belief in the last chamber or closet that makes us feel the best is yet to be, that there is hope and if we only be patient a little longer happiness will come peeking round the corner."

Setarcos stopped and Tommy took the opportunity to ask a question: "How shall I open the last closet?" he asked.

"That's what I was coming to," replied the hag, "You will never open the last closet and you must be thankful that that is the case. As long as there is another chamber to open you will feel there is still hope and that life is worth living. To know yourself completely is to abandon hope and accept life in all its futility. All human progress is rooted in discontent and the fact that the final closet remains forever shut."

"That's quite enough of your pessimistic twaddle," cried Tommy wacking the foot of the philosopher. "Tell me how I can be happier than I am now. Tell me how I can open the before last closet."

"It may already be open. You must take no chances in case an accident should happen and by some misfortune you open the last chamber. Be happy as you are."

"Fat lot of good it is telling me that. I'm unhappy now and I don't want to remain as I am, and all you can say is be happy as you are. It doesn't make sense."

"Oh yes it does. It's because you're trying to open the last closet that you're unhappier than you need be. If you accepted yourself as you are you'd find things more bearable than you do. As it is you're struggling hard to discover a secret which fortunately for you, you will never find.",

"Oh no. And how do you know what I'll find or won't find?"

"I don't know, but I am Setarcos: I have much experience and great knowledge. There is no person wiser than me."

"Bah! What do I care for your credentials. I want to learn something from you and you have taught me nothing. You're just a silly old bore with a lot of talk and nothing to say." The hag jumped to her feet but Tommy went on: "All you can do is to carp away on the same old nonsense; closets and chambers opening and shutting. I don't believe a word of it. You're just a great big fat fraud and I'm glad I found you out."

Tommy did not finish his sentence, for the hag flung a fist at him. He ducked and sprang at her with his cosh uplifted. But she nimbly dodged to one side and punched him on the nose. He fell to the ground unconscious.

A little later when he came to, the hag was gone and nowhere to be seen. Tommy felt distinctly glum. More so than he need have been, for he seemed to think if Setarcos couldn't tell him how or where to find happiness nobody could. He sighed, wiped away a few tears and went out into the street to resume his search. For a while he wandered aimlessly.

Presently he came across a snake that he would have undoubtedly tripped over if it hadn't suddenly jerked its head up in front of him. "Look where you're going you silly man," it hissed.

Tommy gave a start and apologized: "I'm so sorry. I didn't see you all curled up there.'"

"You've got eyes haven't you? Why don't you use them?"

"I've got lots of worries. I don't know whether I'm coming or going, Please forgive my carelessness."

The snake hissed and spat and abused Tommy mercilessly. Eventually, relieved of its venom, it asked him what he was worrying about.

"I'm looking for happiness and nobody seems to know where I can find it. Do you, good Mr Snake, by any chance, know where I can find it?"

The snake did not answer, but with a twist of its neck beckoned the youth to follow it. Tommy, being a courageous lad and believing that everything in life should be given at least one try, did as he was bid. They went up little cobbled tracks, through dark and smelly alleyways and around one bend after another, To Tommy the journey seemed endless, but that was only because he was filled with anticipation and the minutes passed slowly as though they were moments of suffering. "How much further?" he would ask every now and again, but the snake never replied and went wriggling on. Eventually, however, it stopped in an almost dark room. It pointed to the figure in the corner. "She will give you all you want." it hissed.

The woman was robed in black from head to foot and her face was long and wrinkled, very white, with a nose like a parrot. Tommy gave her a suspicious look. "Can you give me happiness?" he asked dubiously.

"No," she replied.

The youth turned angrily to the snake: "You've brought me here under false pretenses you wicked snake. This woman is no more able to give me happiness than any of the other nitwits I've met."

"Oh yes she is. She can give you gold and with gold you can have all the things you want: You can have magnificent palaces and beautiful gardens; delicious food and excellent wines, man servants and maid servants, and any of the other wonderful things God has created to make man happy. There'll be nothing you desire and with all your desires satisfied you'll be happy."

Tommy looked at the witch quizzically. "Is that true?" he asked.

She answered in a high pitched croak: "I will give you gold if you bring me stones. I will pay you by weight. For every pound of stones you bring me you shall receive a pound of gold."

"That sounds fair enough," said Tommy, "but tell me what will you do with the stones?"

"Have I asked you what you will do with the gold?'"

"No, but I can think of more things to do with gold than with stones."

The woman did not reply and so Tommy went on to remind her that she had not answered his first question: "Will gold bring me happiness?"

"I don't know." she replied.

"Has it made the other people you've given it to happy?"

"Gold has never made anybody happy that I know of. People can live comfortably with it, but if they are happy it is not because of it but in spite of it."

"Rubbish," spat the snake. "Gold is money and money is the sixth sense: you can't use the other five without it."

"Yes, but the more money you have the more you want, There's no end to it. You know the saying 'the appetite grows in feeding'. Well, it's the same with gold. Its possession breeds the desire for more. And so it goes on — more and more and more."

"Sssssass… Don't listen to her. You can't possibly know whether gold will bring you happiness until you've had some."

The witch shook her fist angrily. "Enough of your wickedness evil one. Go, before you tempt me to corrupt this youth as you have corrupted me.

The snake, either bored by the discussion or possibly satisfied with itself, did not reply, but curled up on the floor and went to sleep. Poor Tommy by this time was quite bewildered. He glanced from witch to snake as though uncertain who to believe. He wrestled with thought until the sweat stood an his brow. Eventually he asked the witch why she was prepared to give him gold if she knew it wouldn't make him happy.

"Because I want stones, that's why."

"Of course, silly of me to forget. But tell me have you thought of collecting them yourself?"

"Yes naturally. But like you I'm lazy. If I can get somebody else to do my dirty work why shouldn't I?"

"That's right," agreed Tommy and then asked how doing her dirty work made him lazy?

"You're not prepared to earn your own gold are you?"

"I'd never make enough."

"What then makes you think you deserve more than you can earn?"'

Tommy sighed. He was beginning to find the witch tedious. He changed the subject: "Why do you think giving me gold will corrupt me?" he asked.

"Because you will get into bad habits and it will be hard to get rid of them."

"Why should that worry you?"

"It doesn't."

"You're a wicked woman," Tommy cried heatedly. "You're prepared to act against your beliefs just to get stones. That's really bad." He shook head sadly: "If I didn't want your gold I don't think I'd have anything to do with you. I think you're quite the most despicable woman I've ever met."

The witch laughed. "I'm not as bad as all that you know. Really I don't think I'm a wit worse than the politician, businessman, artist, who sacrifices his integrity for the sake of fame or fortune. Or both. We all have to prostitute ourselves in some way or other to get what we want. If we didn't we'd never be able to pander to our vices. I won't deny it: my vice is collecting stones; I'll do anything to get them, but you mustn't think that because of that I'm wicked. I'm not. I'm quite normal, just like everybody else. When you're a bit older you'll understand."

"Never."

"I think you will you know. After all you're not very different from me now. Already I think you're quite prepared to do anything for happiness and who is to say whether it is better to prostitute oneself for that rather than stones or anything else?"

Tommy was too bewildered to reply. Instead he thrust a hand in his pocket and gripped his cosh firmly. He would have struck the woman there and then, but something held him back and he remained still.

"I'll be ready to do business whenever you like," said the witch.

"Well I won't. I'll have nothing to do with your filthy gold so there."

The witch cocked her head to one side. "Pity. You'll never know whether gold could have brought you happiness or not."

Tommy pushed his tongue out at her, but she didn't see because it was dark. He groped his way towards the door. There was a horrid squelchy sound as he accidentally trod on the snake. He stopped, but everything was quiet. He assumed the snake dead and the witch asleep. He slipped out of the sinister room.

As he wended his way back through the dark and smelly alleyways and over the rutted tracks he began to reason with himself: "Perhaps I was wrong to refuse the witch's offer? What does it matter if her gold is corrupt? After all it's not important how one acquires wealth: it's how one uses it that matters. And then the woman is quite right when she says I've got to have gold before I know whether it can bring me happiness. Anyway, youth is the time for experiment: I must experience a little corruption, evil, wickedness, otherwise I'll never know good from bad, right?" And thus Tommy soon persuaded himself he would have to return to the witch for some of her gold.

And so in due course Tommy became a multi-millionaire. He bought a palace and a garden and lived in splendid luxury. There was nothing he deprived himself of. He surrounded himself with fine things and was always ready to pay for the best. He wore lovely clothes tailored in Saville Row, and at table ate this and that delicacy served with the most excellent wines. He had man servants and maid servants who pandered his every need and at night he made love to beautiful virgins. His life was a merry-go-round of pleasure and idleness and he was the envy of all who knew or heard of him.

"He must be the happiest man alive," people would say.

"He must be the shrewdest man alive," others would cynically observe.

"Nobody knows how he makes his money."

And it was in this vein that for a while people talked about him. The witch had prophesied that gold by itself wouldn't bring happiness and in this she was right, for Tommy was, in this regard, like everybody else. He soon tired of luxury and splendor. He became accustomed to fine things and the novelty of good food and wine quickly wore off. He grew bored and restless.

"What shall I do?" he asked the witch one day when she was weighing out the stones he had brought her.

She gave him a sinister look. "The best palliative to boredom is excitement. You must enjoy yourself as much as you can."

And very soon Tommy was under the spell of the witch and developed all manner of bad habits. He took to drink and delighted in its effects rather than its flavor; he gambled and because he was nearly always drunk lost vast sums of money; at night he indulged in wild orgies that even the Borgias would probably have found entertaining. He went from bad to worse. His expenses grew and he had frequent recourse to the witch's gold. She, shrewd woman that she was, soon put her prices up: at first she asked double what he gave her, but then as time passed she demanded three, four and five pounds of stone for every pound of gold. Tommy grew most unhappy and the more unhappy he became the more excitement he sought.

"You can't go on like this, you'll kill yourself," said Rashid the Indian Swami to him one day. Tall, emaciated through fasting, dressed in only a loin cloth this man had come into Tommy's life when he wanted to see a yogi.

"Death doesn't worry me," said Tommy listlessly. "We all have to die some time. The ordeal is the same when you come to it. It doesn't matter if you die a bit sooner or a bit later does it? What difference?"

"You might at least try and be as happy as you can while you're alive."

"Certainly. I couldn't agree with you more. If I'm going to be unhappy in any case I intend to be unhappy in the utmost comfort."

The Swami laughed. "Magnificent reply. The only thing wrong with it is you've decided to be unhappy before you start." Tommy gave him a puzzled look, but the Swami took no notice and continued: "Don't you see that it's all this comfort that is making you unhappy? What you need is discipline. It is not by gratifying your passions you'll find peace but by controlling them."

Tommy scowled. "I don't like discipline," he said, then added with a twinkle in his eye: "I'm build for comfort and not for hardship. Anyway what good would it do me? After all, whatever I do my inner life remains quite unchanged."

The Swami ignored the remark and suggested he get a job.

"A job?" said Tommy incredulously.

"Yes, a job. It will do you the world of good."

"I wouldn't know what to do."

"Do anything, but don't remain idle. Idleness is the thief of time."

"That may be true for you, but it certainly isn't true for me. I'm not in the least bit conscious of time. I've no hopes, ambitions, lofty ideals. I'm not going anywhere. It's only when you're going somewhere that time means anything," He threw his hands up with an air of resignation and then went on: "Yesterday, today, tomorrow — they are only words. They don't mean very much. One day is very much like another."

"If that's how you feel you must be perfectly happy, for you can live the moment."

"Not at all. Most of the time I have a sort of dead feeling

inside. It's precisely because I don't really feel alive that I want to forget myself. Why else do you think I do all the things I do?"

The Swami smiled. "I don't know, but I'm glad you're aware of yourself, that your reason is intact. That's half the battle I'm sure."

"If only you were right. But you couldn't be more wrong. Of what use is reason if the heart points to no signposts? Reason may tell me the best way to Marble Arch, bus or tube, but if my heart doesn't tell me where to go what use is my reason?"

The Swami gave a despairing sigh and abandoned the discussion. He knew from experience that there was no arguing with moods. 'I'll wait until he's in a more optimistic frame of mind,' he said to himself.

The years passed. Every now and again the Swami made a vain attempt to persuade Tommy to alter his ways, but it was no good: the young man remained incorrigible. "I am as I am and there's nothing I can do about it," he would say.

Tommy was now twenty five. He was tall and fair (perhaps even fairer than he had been as a little boy), but his eyes no longer sparkled as they had done then; instead they had a melancholy look about them as though not quite alive. His features, at one time symmetrical, now began to appear slightly incongruous. The forehead, broad and high, was good; but the cheeks were flabby and the mouth undisciplined so that the overall impression was of an intelligent, but dissipated young man.

People thought Tommy would never change and in this opinion he agreed. But then Eureka, something happened. An event occurred which altered the whole circumstances of his life. The witch died. Tommy, who had been intelligent enough to envisage this possibility, but too lazy to do anything about it, went bankrupt. The news quickly spread and people with relish prophesied his doom.

"He's finished." "It won't be long before he's in the gutter." '"He'll probably kill himself when he realizes what a state he's in." "Well, if he doesn't do that he'll end up in the workhouse or the loony bin." "My bet is he'll take to crime, be caught and then detained at Her Majesty's pleasure: anyway, I'm sure that whatever happens to him it will be ugly."

And so people, friends and foe alike, waited for Tommy's downfall, for according to all the laws of nature he had to end badly.

Nothing of the kind however. The witch died and with her, her spell. Once again Tommy became his old self. He quickly abandoned his life of luxury, idleness, dissipation, and resumed his eternal search.

'The first thing I'll do,' he said to himself 'is to go to a harvest camp. The Swami is right. Discipline is what I need. It's only by curbing my passions that I'll achieve the happiness I want.'

Tommy gave up what little wealth he had and set off north to a harvest camp. He had a hundred and fifty miles to go and he determined to walk as transport was a luxury and walking was discipline and that's what he needed.

He had not been going long when he came across a fair. He wouldn't have stopped but the following notice caught his attention:

WORLD FAMOUS TRIO
The Astounding Zen
The Fantastic General Mumbo
The Incredible Prime Minister Jumbo
(One time advisers to the Court Of King WasiWasiland)
ALL YOUR QUESTIONS ANSWERED
Amazing Revelations
Consult Zen Mumbo Jumbo
PRICE 1/-

Tommy paid his shilling and went into the tent. At a table sat three men. On the right General Mumbo, fierce looking with angry emerald eyes and in a bright red uniform with rows upon rows of ribbons and medals dangling from his breast. Next to him sat Zen, small, complacent and by the look of him, apparently happy. He was wearing grey flannels and blazer. The Prime Minister on the other hand gave a different impression. He wore blue jeans, open necked shirt, peaked cap, but had the manners and accent of an Oxford professor. From his looks it was impossible to determine much about him. He could have been anything from a talented dustman to an eccentric Lord.

Tommy hesitantly sat on the stool facing Zen, Mumbo, Jumbo, "Now where can I find happiness?" he asked.

Pause.

The General glared. Zen meditated. The Prime Minister smiled.

Eventually General Mumbo grinned ferociously. "Become a soldier."' he said.

Tommy gave a bewildered look. "How will that make me happy?"

The General grunted. "You're an ignorant man. Surely you've heard of Charles Darwin? At your age I had his book next to my bed instead of the Bible. Knew it like the back of my hand." He coughed and then continued: "If I was a dictator I'd make it compulsory reading in all schools." He nodded his head approvingly. "A great man was Darwin. A very great man."

"Yes, yes, quite. But what's he got to do with becoming a soldier?"

"Plenty. A soldier is in love with death. His job is to kill. And by killing he increases the amount of happiness of those who live."

"Baloney," cried Prime Minister Jumbo thumping his fist on the table. "Death is death and can never bring happiness."

Mumbo ignored the interruption: "The more people you have in the world the unhappier everybody will be. Darwin saw that clearly. If you want to increase human happiness the way to do it is to have less people in the world!" He flashed his teeth gleefully. "Kill'. Kill! Kill! That's what we must do," The Prime Minister tried to say something but the General went booming on: "I became a soldier because it is an honorable profession, most honorable. What can be more noble than to devote one's life to increasing human happiness?"

Tommy had no time to say anything for the Prime Minister piped up: "I've heard all that before. Conservative gibberish, that's what it is. You're no more eager to increase human happiness than a monopolist is to increase the number of his competitors. All you want to do is to perpetuate the vice, wickedness and human folly that has always existed. You teach the young to be like you and then, God help us, they turn out like you. If you want to see the fruits of your work, General Mumbo, look around you. Look around you. You will see nothing but misery and suffering inflicted on man by man."

"Yes, but only because idiots like you seek to deny nature's laws. The world was made for the strong and powerful. The weak and feeble are nature's accidents. It is right that they should be destroyed for they are no good and , like the dead leaves of a plant, suck the vitality from the vigorous and healthy. It is not me, but you with your foolish notions of human betterment that perpetuate the misery of the weak and deny the strong the happiness which is their due."

"Phoooee," squealed the Prime Minister. "There are no strong or weak except those that man himself creates. All men are equal: one man is a poet, another a carpenter, yet another a dustman, clergyman or teacher. Who is to say they are not equal?"

The General gave a contemptuous snort.

Jumbo went on: "Already we've made immense progress. We have equality of religious worship; equality before the law;

equality of the sexes; political equality, and now we are fighting hard for equality between nations and equal opportunity for all. All this is an excellent thing I say, but it is not enough. You can't have equality before the law, political equality or equal opportunity unless you have economic equality first. This is where I come in. I'm a pioneer in a new movement. I say that every man, woman and child must get equal pay regardless of the work he or she does. Only then will there be universal happiness and respect of man for man."

The General crashed a fist on the table. "Stuff of nonsense," he thundered. "Nobody would be happy in your foolish Utopia. The weak would hate it for they'd know they were getting more than they deserved; and the strong would hate it because it would be unjust and they'd be getting less than they deserved. You can't strengthen the feeble by weakening the strong."

"Oh yes you can. If there were no inequalities everybody would do their fair share. As it is the poor can't and the rich won' t. The poor can't because they're underfed, underclothed and overworked. The rich won't because they're overfed, over-clothed and under-worked. It's as simple as that."

"Bah, you foolish dreamer. If only you'd read Darwin you wouldn't talk such rubbish. You ought to know that no good can come from helping the poor. Improve their lot and what happens? They breed; and instead of making them better off you've made them worse off. It's plain logic. The facts are irrefutable." He stopped. He looked well pleased with himself. Then, just when Jumbo was going to interrupt, he added: "Anyway, if the poor weren't poor they'd never do any work. The only way to keep them at it is to under-feed them, under-pay them and keep them so busy that they haven't time to reproduce."

"Ughl" grunted the Prime Minister ant then squeaked excitedly: "It's no use discussing anything with you. You see and hear only what you want to see and hear. You're a hundred years behind the times and I'm a hundred years ahead of them. What did Darwin know of birth control, modern science, sociology?" He did not wait for a reply but continued: "Precisely nothing. And you persist in spouting his silly old theories just because you're too lazy to think up any new ones yourself. You're like all those university trained idiots who have to learn other peoples' ideas because they're quite incapable of having any of their own."

The General laughed. "Your insults will not hurt me," he retorted with dignity. "I am no idle dreamer. I see and hear things as they are. I don't feed my mind with gluttonous fantasies when starving realities are all around me." He stroked his belly affectionately. "I'm a realist if ever there was one."

"Realist indeed!" shouted the Prime Minister. "There's no such animal. Reality is man's greatest fiction. When you say you're a realist all you mean is that you're an old-fashioned noodle whose beliefs are exactly the same as everybody else's."

"Nonsense," barked the General.

"Nonsense yourself," squawked the Prime Minister. "I know what I'm saying. I'm a great man and the strength of a great man is his everlasting inability to adapt himself to reality. The difference between small fry and big fry is that small fry adapts to the status quo (which they call reality) and big fry alter it, mold it to their vision, which is what I am doing."

Mumbo snorted and was about to say something when Tommy jumped up waving his arms around. "Enough of this twaddle," he cried. "I didn't pay a shilling for nothing. Tell me how I can find happiness." He paused, then addressed Zen. "Isn't it about time you said something? What do you think of all this mumbo jumbo?"

"Admirable. The best shillings worth of entertainment you'll get anywhere. If you give them half a chance they'll go an forever.

Tommy gave a look of quiet despair. "Do you mean to say they'll never agree with each other?"

"Of course," replied Zen and then grinned a little more: "They're like our famous leaders: they agree to disagree. It's what you'd expect isn't it? The show must go on. If they agreed they'd never keep you interested. And we get bored so quickly don't we? No, I haven't finished. I can guess what you're going to say. Yes, I know that leaders sometimes agree, but you mustn't take that seriously. It's all part of the game. They'll agree with each other on minor points, pretend they don't and then to show how clever they are, agree with each other in the finale." He threw up his hands as though he had just expounded a theorem. "Clever isn't it?"

Tommy grunted and asked Zen if he was happy.

"Perfectly. I'm the happiest man alive."

"I don't see how you can be when you're such a cynic."

"Well I am."

"What is your secret?"

The other reflected and then replied somewhat ambiguously: "When I eat I eat; when I sleep I sleep; when I do nothing I do nothing; when I am generous I am generous; when I am cynical I am cynical.'"

"Yes, yes. I understand. No. no, no I didn't mean that. I don't understand at all. Explain yourself."

"I will tell you a little story," said Zen and this is what he told him:

Everybody in the small town of C___ took great pride in their beautiful little opera house, for they loved opera. There were many amateur starlets in the little town, but none with any real talent so that it was an important and happy occasion when famous stars from the great capitals of the world came and sung at their opera house.

Now there existed three bad men in this town who were forever on the lookout for a quick and easy way of making a fortune. Up till now they had never been very successful and they were barely able to afford the necessities which enabled them to pass as respectable citizens. But one day one of them had a bright idea: "Let us engage a French troupe to sing at our opera house," he said. "We can hire the building and we'll make a fortune," He then explained his plan.

When he had finished the others smiled and murmured agreement.

Soon the whole town knew that a famous French troupe would be coming. People rejoiced and then quickly hurried to the box office for tickets.

"Alas! All sold out," said the little man at the office and then after a pause whispered confidentially: "If you go round the corner there is, I think, a man who might be able to sell you tickets"

"Thank you. Thank you," each opera loving person would cry and hurry round the corner to buy tickets from a little man who sold them at five times the official price!

Time passed. The first night was approaching. Everybody was very excited. Happiness seemed to throb in the air. Husbands and wives no longer screamed at each other. Those undergoing analysis gave it up, as though miraculously cured. People who hadn't been on the best of terms smiled and greeted each other, and in some cases even had tea together. C_____ was a happy place to live in.

Then suddenly everything changed. A tragedy hit the town. The French troupe, due to unforseen circumstances, was unable to come. The three bad men, who were of course good men in the eyes of the citizens of C_____, immediately reassured everybody that tickets would be refunded in full.

Everybody hurried along to the opera house to salvage whatever funds they could, and the three bad men gladly reimbursed all those with tickets, for they didn't want to lose their respectability and they had never expected to more than quadruple their money on the official price of a seat.

Tommy grunted. "Yes, all very nice, but what's it got to do with happiness?"

Zen beamed. "What were you thinking about when I was telling you my story?"'

"I wasn't thinking about anything. I was listening to you."

"And you're sure you weren't thinking of anything else?"

"Positive."

"There you are then. You know the secret of happiness. You don't have to be taught." But poor Tommy looked so bewildered that Zen went on: "Wholeheartedness is the secret of happiness. To do everything with all your might. To keep nothing in reserve. To let nothing go to waste. When a person lives like that he is said to be the golden haired lion. He is the symbol of unity, sincerity, wholeheartedness. He is divinely human."

"Yes, but that doesn't tell me how I can become wholehearted?"

Zen did not reply but got up from his stool and went out of the tent.

"Well of all the cheek!" exclaimed Tommy jumping to his feet. "I've never seen such rudeness in all my life. Why didn't he want to answer my question?"

"Because he can't," replied Mumbo and Jumbo together. The General then added: "He always leaves when he can't answer a question."

"He's a coward," tittered the Prime Minister. "He's so interested in himself that he's got no time to be interested in anybody else."

There was a pause, and then Tommy, glancing from Mumbo to Jumbo, like a spectator at a tennis tournament, asked what he should do.

"Become a soldier," cried the General.

"Noooooooooo," howled the Prime Minister. "Become a reformer and establish equality for all."

"Reduce the world's population," Mumbo boomed.

"Strengthen the weak: weaken the strong," squealed Jumbo.

"Destroy the weak: strengthen the strong?" thundered the General. "Read Darwin and see for yourself."

"Read Marx and learn the truth."

This interchange might have gone on forever if the General had not believed that the sword was mightier than the pen. He took out his revolver and shot Jumbo straight through the heart. Tommy quickly snatched his old and faithful cosh from his pocket and pouncing on the General began beating him on the head. "Take that," he cried. "And that; and that, you wicked murderer." Mumbo flopped to the ground with no more dignity than a private.

Tommy was immediately grabbed by two strong security guards. Zen and Jumbo dashed to the rescue of their dear friend, the General.

"You'll pay for this," screamed Jumbo. "Nobody is going to hurt a friend of mine and get away with it. "

"You've ruined our show," cried Zen with an un-Zen-like screech.

"Kill him,"'mumbled the half dying General.

The two security guards lifted Tommy bodily off his feet, as though he was no heavier than a fly and carried him outside the tent, and with two good kicks on the backside sent him flying into a nearby field.

After a while Tommy got up and brushing the dirt off his clothes resumed his march north. At the harvest camp he did not spare himself. He worked from dawn to dusk, first in the fields and later on the threshing machines and in the granaries. Sun or rain he kept at it, and no doubt would have gone on doing so, but the wind and cold warned him of approaching winter and work began to slacken off. The farmers started sacking the casual laborers they had taken on for the summer, and in due course Tommy drifted down to London once again.

There he tried everything. He became a salesman for six months and made good money; but what was the use of money if it didn't bring him happiness? He was a school teacher for a little while longer, but eventually gave that up too as he felt it wrong to teach when he didn't know anything himself. Then he became a librarian, social worker, taxi driver, barman, waiter, postman, docker, grave digger, and a few other things too. None of them answered his needs. He quickly tired, grew bored, listless and ineffective. If he learnt anything at all from these experiences it was that self-discipline (in the sense of forcing yourself to do something you didn't really want to do) made you mean, petty and vicious. What's more, it was folly to expect others to appreciate your self-sacrifice.

Tommy was now thirty. He looked vigorous and strong and gave the impression of a man in his prime. But appearances were deceptive. Tommy was in the lowest of spirits. He was more unhappy than he had ever been, for now he seemed to think that happiness didn't exist. And further, that all his efforts had been futile. In this mood of self-pity he began to ask himself a different sort of question: "Why do I live?" "What is my purpose in life?" "Have I one?" "And if so, will finding it bring me happiness?" Day and night these questions haunted him. He became obsessed with them, and because he found no answers, concluded that there were none. He resolved to kill himself.

Various possibilities crossed his mind. Gas? No: it was too complicated and often failed... Poison? No: that was useless because he hadn't any and didn't see a way of getting some. He thought of shooting himself, but that was difficult without a gun. Then he contemplated throwing himself off a bridge, but instantly rejected the idea as he imagined he would be rescued and then forced to serve a prison sentence for attempted suicide!... Electrocution? Useless: that was scientific and he hadn't a scientific mind... He could cut his veins open while in the bath, that he had heard was a pleasant (pleasant is perhaps the wrong word) way to die. But that was messy. Then, it struck him that he wouldn't have to clear the mess up. Tommy continued to ruminate, and no doubt would have gone on doing so until something or other prompted him to make a decision.

One fine day, however, while walking in Kensington Gardens, he was abruptly jolted from the thoughts that forever preoccupied him. "Why are you so glum? Is not life beautiful?" said a tender, beautiful voice.

He looked up and saw a strange looking girl. He blinked as he could hardly believe his eyes. The girl had long flowing fair hair almost down to her waist. She wore large mauve sun glasses (though it wasn't that bright) and in one hand she held a daisy. Her garb was hip — blue jeans, brown leather jacket, green cardigan. She was smiling pleasantly.

"What do you want?'"he asked.

"For you." And she presented him the flower. He took it and held it as though the stem had been the tail of a rat.

"Isn't it beautiful?" she said.

"It's just an ordinary daisy."

"It's quite unique. There's not another one like it in the whole world... But you still haven't told me why you are so glum?"

"It's nothing," he grunted. But he was beyond caring and told her the truth: "All my life I have searching for happiness. I have consulted the great and the small, the wise and the foolish, the rich and ... and many many other people. None have been able to answer my question and I have come to believe there is no answer." Then he felt an old stirring within his breast and the familiar words poured out almost as though he was reciting a lesson. "Perhaps you can tell me where I can find happiness? You seem content enough."

She gave him a look of surprise. "Is that the question you've been asking all your life?"

He nodded.

Her face paled. "You poor man," she cried. "You have been under the influence of the devil. You've never asked the right question."

"Oh! What should that be?'"

"Have you never loved?"

"No, I don't think so. I don't think I'm capable of it.",

"That's silly. Everybody is capable of love. Has nobody ever loved you?"

"Lots of people have said they loved me. But what does that amount to? As I see it, all it means is that somebody or other loves their illusion of you." He gave a sinister chuckle. "And as though that wasn't enough they proceed to make your life quite unbearable by expecting you to live up to that illusion… No, no if that's love I've had quite enough of it."

"I love you,'" she said gently. "But I love you as you are."

"How can you love me? You don't even know me."

"I love everything and everybody."

"That's nonsense," protested Tommy. "You can't possibly."

"How shall I GIVE happiness should have been your question."

There was a very long silence.

Eventually Tommy asked Christine (that was her name) how he could give happiness.

She smiled. "Why don't you let me live with you and see for yourself?"

He looked her up and down. His lips twitched. He didn't know what to say. She divined his thoughts: "I have a beautiful body, but my soul is more beautiful."

"What is soul?"

"I will teach you if you will let me?"

Tommy had nothing to lose and agreed.

The two young people moved into a cubicle of a flat in Bloomsbury.

They hadn't many possessions, but soon there were

paintings on the walls, brightly colored drapes, ornaments of one description or another, flowers, plants, pretty lamp shades. Christine was always puttering around—decorating, mending, cooking. She laughed; she sung; she listened; she didn't talk too much. During the day she worked in a boutique. Tommy did one job, then another and another, then several others. Often he did nothing. He berated himself for his instability, his inability to find a niche. But he no longer contemplated suicide. Somehow with Christine around some of her cheerfulness rubbed off on to him.

Then one day, quite unexpectedly, she told him she was leaving him.

"No,'"he protested the blood draining from his face.

"Yes," she said. "I've got myself a new boy friend."

"But don't you love me any more?"

"Of course I do; but I love him too."

"How can you love both of us."

"I love everybody." And she gave him an affectionate hug. "You'll soon find yourself another girl. There are plenty around."

He sat down on the sofa and began weeping.

"Don't cry. Don't cry Tommy," she said. "I was only joking. I just wanted to see if you loved me."

He looked up, smiling, wiping the tears from his eyes. "Of course I love you. I can't live without you." Then he grabbed her and smacked her playfully on the rump. "I want to marry you."

"I'm nothing special you know. Soon I'll be old and wrinkled and fat."

"Not to me. It's you I love, not your body," Then he added lightly: "Though I like that too."

And so Christine and Tommy got married. They settled down to a quiet family life. Soon they were able to buy a house in the country and because it was filled with love it was a beautiful house and a happy home for their children.